Wedding Night

Wedding Night

Yusuf Abu Rayya

Translated by
R. Neil Hewison

The American University in Cairo Press
Cairo   New York

English translation copyright © 2006 by
The American University in Cairo Press
113 Sharia Kasr el Aini, Cairo, Egypt
420 Fifth Avenue, New York 10018
www.aucpress.com

Copyright © 2002 by Yusuf Abu Rayya
First published in Arabic in 2002 as *Laylat 'urs*
Protected under the Berne Convention

Dar el Kutub No. 23661/05
ISBN-10: 977 416 006 1
ISBN-13: 978 977 416 006 6

Designed by Sally Boylan/AUC Press Design Center
Printed in Egypt

You are blind, and I am deaf and dumb, so let our hands touch
that we may understand each other.

Jibran Khalil Jibran, Sand and Foam

Since I am prepared for the wedding,
Like a goose on a plate,
Let the celebrations begin.
Let the murderers and sodomites dance
With the kings and the saints.
Let the prostitutes bless this marriage instead of the priests,
So that this night may have beautiful issue.
Let the celebrations begin,
Because I am completely prepared,
Like the wedding chests.

Wadie Saada, The Feast

Wedding Preparations

1

Blind Amin climbed the minaret of the market mosque. His glorifications fell from the sky of the neighborhood and drifted among the closed windows and doors of the houses; hearts shivered in awe.

"Praised be He Who was named before He was named."

"Praised be He Whose throne is upon the water."

"Praised be He Who taught Adam the names of things."

Zaki tossed for some time in his bed, and when he heard the call to prayer he rose to turn up the wick of the lamp a little so that the phantoms of the room took shape, dark forms scattered here and there: a tattered reed mat, a fetid old quilt, a water pot with water seeping around its base, a zinc urn with a tap that dripped all night long into a small jug, echoing the slumbering heartbeats.

He splashed his dark face with a little water, bent over to the skirt of his gallabiya to dry himself, then went to the corner of the room dense with shadows. He shook Houda's shoulder, and when there was no response kicked him in the rear. But the curled body did not unfold, so he was obliged, as every morning, to fill his palm with water and sprinkle it on Houda's face. Now Houda leaped up screeching, "Ab . . . ab!"

Zaki raised his hand to his ear to let him know that Amin had made the dawn call to prayer. Then he signaled to him again with both hands to indicate that today was market day and that they must make the most of their time before the crowds in order to reach the maallim's shop before sunrise.

Houda replied that he understood all this—and he tried to curl up again, placing his head on his folded arm. But Zaki did not let him—he pulled him by his other arm and dragged him to the tap, bending his head down under it so that the water fell on his coarse hair, while he squirmed and screamed in a muffled voice, "Ab . . . ab!"

He was obliged to wipe his face with his sleeves. Then he bent down to his tools—knives, cleavers, long files, thick ropes, and large metal bowls—and picked them up under his arm, before arranging some of them on the leather belt tied around his waist.

Zaki blew into the openings at the bottom of the lamp, and the flame flickered and choked. He blew again and black smoke rose and circled inside the dark glass, and the flame was extinguished.

Now they were outside the room, which was set apart on its own. In front of it was a narrow space, overlooked by the walls of another room, whose door opened on the opposite side and whose occupant was a student at the religious institute. He was from a remote village, and he studied Quran and Hadith, as well as the most difficult reaches of rhetoric and grammar. He was long past the age for studying, but his father had insisted that he finish his education and earn the secondary certificate so that he could be accepted at al-Azhar University in Cairo. Thus he dreamed, and thus he had given his son to God and to His Glorious Quran as he caressed the covering of the Kaaba on his one and only pilgrimage to Mecca. He bent his head and clutched the blessed black covering next to the Black Stone, and allowed his tears to flow as he sobbed, "If You bless me with a son I will dedicate him to Your Glorious Book."

When the young man faltered in his studies, his father had begun the process of marrying him off. He engaged him to a girl from the village, who now lived in the family house while the young man went alone to the town to attend the institute and find the time to accumulate his knowledge.

He was fiddling with the lock of his room when they came out.

"Good morning, ya mawlana."

"Peace and the mercy of God and his blessings. May God grant you your licit daily bread."

He went off ahead of them with his lame gait, leaning his hand on his good leg, dragging the paralyzed one, which had never developed and was no bigger than a small child's.

Across the way was the door of Umm Ali, the owner of the rooms and the two-story house. She rented out the lower rooms, and lived with her four daughters on the upper floor.

Houda signaled to his brother that he wanted to urinate in the shared lavatory of Umm Ali's house. Zaki replied that they would call in at the mosque, as every morning, but Houda indicated in agony that he could not wait and that he would wet himself, so Zaki said, "Go on, then."

He pushed him in and stood waiting for him at the door that connected the rooms to Umm Ali's house, observing the sleeping street. Houda went into the stairwell and pushed open the door of the lavatory, where he found Fikri the housepainter straining his body as he squatted, supporting himself with both hands against the walls. He screeched apologetically, "Ab . . . ab!"

He stepped back to watch the open door, as his mute self whispered, "My God, how can what I dreamed come true?"

This is how he had seen her shortly before Zaki woke him, in this same loose red dress with the fluffy trim around the collar that began thick and luxuriant at the back of the neck and ended light and slender at the navel, leaving plenty of room for the movement of the ample breasts. Now she was here in front of him, just as he had seen her in his dream. She was bending

7

over to pull the bucket and brush out from under the big black bed with the transparent mosquito net suspended from its four posts.

Fakiha was conscious of the wide eyes that were staring intensely at her. She saw the tears of lust flowing down his cheeks, and her body shook. "What does this idiot want from me? He never stops staring at my whole body. When I'm sitting among the women neighbors he only looks at me. His eyes are like knives tearing my body apart, exposing its secrets. I can't bear their humiliating, shameless, fearless looks."

She came out with her husband's equipment to put it in front of the door, and went back to the room to prepare his breakfast. Houda caught up with her.

"What do you want?" She turned her white palm up in the air to ask the question.

He pointed to where his heart was and lowered his eyelids, then brought his closed fingers to his lips.

"Find yourself someone else."

She heard Fikri calling from the lavatory and was alarmed. Her whole body trembled. "Yes?"

"Have you got the food ready?"

"Yes."

She pushed Houda out, and he backed away without taking his eyes from the two well formed breasts between the pink fluff that rested on the twin mountain of her bosom.

At the door his feet stuck fast to the floor, and he resolved to lunge, the desires of his skinny hand being greater than his will— it wanted to take hold of one of the bulges of this towering, perfectly proportioned, divinely engineered body, a body that would arouse the desire of a suckling babe.

Just as he was about to launch the surprise assault, three things happened:

Fakiha bent down to the brush, whose wooden handle stuck out of the bucket; her husband emerged after dealing with his needs, busy pulling up his trousers and drying his hands on their rainbow-spattered legs; and Shaykha Aida came downstairs, led by her younger sister Nawal.

Fikri gave morning greetings to everyone and signaled to Houda to go into the lavatory, even though he had now retreated outside in defeat, preceded by Nawal, holding her blind sister's hand, on their way to the cemetery to catch the female mourners before the hot sun rose too high, and to return before noon with a great fortune of pastry and bread rolls and a small amount of money.

He was distracted by Nawal's small rump, squeezed into a tight gallabiya that was drawn in at the hips and ran in pleats across the two strong, firm buttocks. His impotent desires awoke once more, and he stepped quickly to walk beside them along the long corridor. In a flash, like a bird of prey tearing with its talons at the throat of a pigeon, he grabbed at the girl's two prominent little lupine seeds, which were bursting into the resplendence of femininity with unsuspected vigor. The child in her was alarmed, and she struck at his claw, soiled with dried blood.

"You dirty thing!"

Shaykha Aida scolded her sister. "Must you really?"

"The mute knocked into me."

"I'll give you a knock!"

Zaki, startled by the events, grabbed his brother by the collar of his blood-caked robe. "Stop getting us into trouble."

Houda held up a finger and wrapped the fingers of the other hand around it, to say, "I keep telling you to get me married."

They went out into the street, and a cool breeze touched their faces. The fresh air made them both cough at the same breath to expel the foul air of the room in viscid phlegm, which they trod into the ground.

9

Fakiha, in her red dress with its soft fluffy trim, continued to picture Houda's eyes for some time afterward. Since her husband had brought her here from her distant village, Fakiha had fascinated the young men of the neighborhood with her tall stature, her soft hair left to fall wild around her shoulders, and her dresses that accentuated many of her charms. She was not like the other women of the quarter, who wore tightly buttoned gallabiyas and black headscarves and went out wearing black slippers of thick leather. She preferred joyful, gaudy colors, she was original in her choice of headscarves bordered with large, bright flowers, and she went out in bright-colored sandals with brilliant roses on the front. She also constantly chewed gum, which she cracked beneath her small white teeth and pushed out with the tip of her tongue to make a pop that shook the fiery hearts of the boys who never tired of loitering under her window or standing for hours under the walls of the big house. The walls stretched from Pottery Street to the cheese factory. Over them hung the green branches of tall mulberry trees, which leaned far out and in the midday heat cast their shade in front of Umm Ali's house.

Fakiha spent the days alone once Fikri had left with his bucket and brushes, his work clothes decorated with the colors of his paints, the deeply ingrained oil stains not quite obliterated from his face. She might go out to run an errand here or there, or to buy vegetables from the market, or she might sit with the women under the walls of the big house.

If Houda saw her as he was coming or going, he could never contain himself—his body would compel him forward and willy-nilly lead him to her. Sometimes his hand would rise up to grasp her fleshy arm constricted in its tight sleeve, and sometimes he would find himself face to face with her, blocking her path, invading her embrace in the narrow passageway of Umm Ali's house.

One day he took leave of his senses when he came back from the butcher's shop to find her bending over at the doorway, her backside high in the air, as she swept up the mulukhiya stalks scattered on the floor inside. He leaped onto her from the doorstep, grabbing both her buttocks and knocking her forcefully forward. Her surprise was so great that she almost fell on her face, just managing to stop herself. She wheeled around to hit him with the broom, but he was not ready to let go, swinging behind her as she turned. In order to get the better of him, she shoved him against the wall, and the "Ow!" he uttered was loud and clear. He cupped his hands between his thighs and ran doubled over, cowering and dejected, to his room. She followed him with the broom in her white hand, merry with its shiny gold bracelets.

Truly furious, she signaled to him that if he did anything like that again she would tell her husband: she raised her free hand to her lip to twirl an imaginary moustache. She would expose him to the residents of the house so that he would be kicked out into the street. And she mimed with the broom toward the door: she would sweep him out like a pile of garbage. Then she would make a scandal of him in front of the whole neighborhood—and she raised both hands to describe a large circle, and kicked the air with her leg, to mean that everyone would cast him out.

He kept his attention on her as he inserted the key in the padlock, contemplating her beauty. He wished he could throw his thin body into her arms, although the pain that rose from below doused his desire. He put his finger to each eye in turn in a gesture of obedience, then bunched his dry, skinny fingers to his lips and launched a kiss into the air. This made her smile and forget her vehement anger. He entered his dark, depressing room satisfied with the smile but regretful of the failure that had thwarted his potency.

11

The two brothers turned right, heading for the main asphalted road, where they would wait for the donkey-cart at the entrance to the station. They passed beyond Umm Ali's house, avoiding the dew that dripped from the mulberry trees of the big house, and neared the house of Abu Sinna, who emerged from its gloom carrying his stinking fish crates.

"Good morning."

"And a fine morning to you."

He rested the crates on the ground after a struggle with the weight of them, and stood wiping the sweat on his forehead. He smiled at Houda and threw his hand in the air in a sign of greeting. Houda returned the greeting carelessly and let out an inarticulate angry grumble that announced his dislike of the man.

"What's the matter?"

"The same as always," replied Zaki.

"It would have been my pleasure, but the girl's still too young."

Houda understood what the man meant and spat toward the mulberry tree whose branches bent over to touch his head. He wanted to pull his brother away and stop him prattling with this man, but Zaki drew him closer and signed to him that he could hear screams and that he knew whose voice it was. Abu Sinna's daughter came rushing out and threw herself into her father's arms.

Her mother ran after her holding a broom in one hand and the girl's wet pants in the other. The father bent over the girl and wrapped her in his arms to protect her from the beating, so that the blows missed their target and dislodged his turban.

"For goodness' sake, woman!"

"She's of an age to be married!"

Zaki felt embarrassed and dragged Houda to be on their way, but Houda pulled away and clapped one hand on the other, as he looked at the sky that had begun to glow with the sunrise of a new day. "Ab . . . ab . . . ."

12

Zaki shoved him in reproval and signed to make him understand, "This is the one you wanted to marry! Be patient for your blessings—you'll find the right girl." Houda showed that he was convinced of this by putting two fingers to each side of his head.

It was an odd haphazard that Abu Sinna's daughter should emerge at this moment and that her mother was prepared to shame her in public. Every day when the two brothers left the house, their eyes fell on the same scene: the father preparing his crates to take them to the main road and stand there with the other fishmongers waiting for the Matariya truck that came from the far north loaded with Nile fish—bulti, bayad, buri, and a few eels. They would see the girl coming out of the depths of the house carrying the baskets and the scales to accompany her father to wherever he was going to sell the fish, whether in the town market or farther afield in the markets of the neighboring towns and villages. She would be preceded by her mother's lofty figure and long limbs, tying up her black headscarf and looking back every now and then to call out to her, "Get a move on, Nadia!"

Behind them, Houda would hurry to keep up so as not to miss the sight of the thrust back buttocks rising and falling with the gait of the girl wearied by the weight of her burden. Had the mother done this on purpose, to put an end to his urgent demands for the girl's hand? Was she really so young that she could not control her bladder? Perhaps.

Zaki signed to him, "Put a waterproof sheet under her like mothers do for their children!"

Houda replied by signing that her young age was no reason for him not to marry her, and that if she developed under his care he would be able to control her and form her as he liked. He brought his hands up to his chest to make a sign of two breasts, then he kissed his bunched fingers to indicate how beautiful the girl was.

13

His brother hushed him in order to return the greeting of a woman carrying a milk pot on her head, on her way to the dairy. She was the first of the neighborhood women to appear—an energetic woman, she milked her animals early and hurried with the warm milk to collect her money and return home to prepare her husband's breakfast before he went off to his fields. Other women followed her, emerging from the side streets with pots on their heads, but there were fewer of them the higher the street rose, until at the oil press and the stone houses that included the grocery stores, the cafés, the restaurants, and the mat-makers' stores, no more were to be seen. The main road was a bustle of cars coming from south and north and meeting at the entrance to the town in a street that narrowed at the iron crossing gates, constricted to a single line of stores and houses facing the railway wall of white rubble that stretched from one end of the town to the other.

This was where the crowds were, and this was where all the roads met. The train station, the bus station, the service taxi rank, the food and bilela carts, the fruit stalls, the newspaper stand, the greatest concentration of cafés, and the donkey mews where the farmers from the surrounding villages left their rides until they returned from their journeys to other towns.

Zaki and Houda approached Mitwalli's café and stood for a while around the fire that rose from the broad brazier, extending their hands to the tongues of flame to warm their cold fingers. Adenoidal Aziza appeared in the weak light that fell onto the counter from the brazier, lighting a fire under the sand box. When she turned around to arrange the tobacco rack she saw the brothers and raised her hand in greeting, winking at Zaki with her good eye. He smiled, but Houda was sullen and turned his back on her. Her coarse voice called out from inside the café, "Is your friend still sulking?"

"Ask him." And he tugged Houda by his gallabiya sleeve to look at her, but Houda wrenched his arm away. He left the patch of light thrown out by the fire and stood facing the iron crossing gates waiting for the donkey-cart. His intestines stirred inside him and he felt nauseous—if his stomach had not been empty, he would have spilled its contents onto the asphalt. He threw down the containers and knives he was carrying on his shoulders and held his belly.

His mind dwelled on this temptress, Adenoidal Aziza the public convenience. Mitwalli had taken her on when she landed in the town for the mulid, finding that she was smart and good at café work. She was a wanderer who pursued her livelihood from mulid to mulid and from town to town, serving in rough cafés and sleeping with whoever wanted her—though wanting her required a special courage, and only the very needy would approach her. She was one-eyed, dark, and scabby, and she smelled of the water she scooped from the café's waste bucket, a brew of rotting honey-tobacco mixed with tea dregs, coffee grounds, and fenugreek seeds, all infused with the stale smoke of the extinguished and discarded corn cobs that were used for lighting the gozas.

Houda would not go near her, despite her repeated forays. When he finished work at the maallim's shop, he and his brother would be awarded one of the livers of the slaughtered animal, and they would stand with it at a small wooden cart in front of Mitwalli's café from nightfall until there was no one left in the street or until the fried liver was all gone. Houda would stand in front of the broad tray, flipping a piece of liver, then removing it with a strainer onto a plate spread with parsley. Zaki would open the loaves and shove into them the required amount of liver after placing it on the scales. Engrossed in his work, Houda would be surprised by the hand grabbing at his genitals, and he would scream. When he turned around he would find Aziza roaring with thick, masculine laughter as she collected the tumblers, plates, and gozas from the customers.

The men would applaud her trick and ask her to repeat it, and she would take her time while waiting for his attention to lapse again. Houda would forget what she had done and would stand once more at the broad tray, flipping the liver, and calling to a customer by raising his palm to the side of his head and screeching, "Beek . . . beek!" Aziza would creep back to pluck at the end of his limp tool, and he would chase after her with the strainer, plunging among the sitting men and into the café. Then Mitwalli would put himself between them, clapping his hand to his chest— "Please, for my sake"—and leaning over to kiss Houda's head.

One time when she played her game, he caught her and pinned her between the wall of the counter and the hot sand box. He held both her arms and shoved at her chest, butting it with his head, but he was surprised to find his erection making its own way to her private parts. Her arms relaxed and fell, their eyes met, and she winked at him. His jaw dropped idiotically as she signaled to him that she would pretend to her husband she needed to go home for something, and that he should follow her.

Houda returned to his brother distracted and unable to keep his body under control. He left the strainer in the oil and signed that he was going to the lavatory in the nearby mosque—because he was desperate—and he would be back in the blink of an eye (pointing to his eyes). Zaki let him go.

He followed Aziza and went through the open door. She emerged from the inner room having taken off her black work gallabiya and released her hair from its eternal headscarf. She left the door ajar and led him by the hand to her bed covered by a faded checked sheet. She sat on the edge of the bed, pulled up her dress, and beckoned him. He approached hesitantly, and as she pulled the dress higher he was astonished to see that she was completely

16

naked underneath it. He stared at what he saw between her thighs and came nearer. She grabbed his arms and pulled him to bend down in front of her. He dropped to his knees, and she put her hands to his head to push his face into her crotch. But when he came close and the coarse hairs touched the tip of his nose, his stomach turned and rose to his gullet. Helplessly, he wrenched his face away and into her belly. She flung him to the ground and kicked at him, and he ran for the door, wiping the sides of his mouth on his sleeve. He headed back to the liver cart, trembling.

His brother noticed the change in his demeanor but did not ask him the reason. Out of the corner of his eye he spotted Aziza returning to work at the café, and his smile broadened. His sides shook as he sang along with the song on the café radio.

Houda signaled to his brother to join him when he saw the donkey-cart coming from the other end of town. It struggled up to the railway crossing, the driver yelling at the donkey to propel it up to the area covered with small black stones on both sides of the tracks.

The brothers approached the cart and climbed onto it, one on each side, after placing their tools in the empty tubs along with the gear of the others sitting around the edges. The cart began making its way down to the street below, as the driver shouted at the women in front, with their baskets large and small overflowing with all kinds of vegetables. "Watch out, woman! Mind your back, lady!"

Smells of dill, parsley, cabbage, and guava wafted around them as the wheels of the cart creaked left and right. The cart swayed in its cautious descent toward the pottery dealers, who had spread their goods on both sides of the road, and did not pick up speed until it left the town and entered the fields that swam in the light mist. Here the donkey felt emancipated and trotted along the asphalt road, crossing bridges built of stone and iron.

It was a long and tiring journey to reach the abattoir, but the fields were splendidly green and the cool fresh air filled the donkey's lungs to capacity, providing them with all the strength and energy they needed.

After the branch canal, the cart turned off to the left so that the maallim's men could join the rest of the butchers. These included the peddlers, who acquired half a carcass—to be hung from a wooden tripod at markets or on the highway—and the tripe merchants, who specialized in offal—head meat, trotters, lights, tripe, and intestines—which they carried in large tubs to their carts in order to sell at the butchers' corner of the town market, to hawk at other markets, or to display on street corners. Then there were the apprentices of the big maallims, who carried a whole carcass on their backs, or sometimes more than one, according to the time of year or the days of the week on which meat was allowed to be sold.

The cart pulled up and Zaki and Houda and the rest of the men got down and joined the throng to enter the gate of the abattoir, passing severed heads, skinned carcasses, and trotters strung on ropes, avoiding the river of blood running along the gutter, and following the carcasses suspended on hooks until they found their workmate who did the slaughtering. He had already finished his task, and he pointed to the maallim's meat for them to take it down from its hook. One of them went in under the split carcass with his shoulder and lifted it slightly to release it. The hanging part tilted over his head, another man seized it, and they carried it off together to the cart waiting outside.

2

Maallim Osman got up and went to the basin to wash his hands and mouth. As she stood beside him holding the towel, straightening the collar of his nightshirt, he saw her evenly parted black hair falling over her snow-white face in the mirror. When he turned to her, he held that face in both hands to gaze at its total beauty and to steal a quick kiss from her lips. She hit him tenderly on the shoulder. "You'll be late for the shop."

She left the towel on his arm and walked away down the wide corridor, taking the breakfast dishes to the kitchen. He gazed at the transparency of the soft, white gown and the distinct dark shadows of her underwear.

What a virgin of paradise! This woman will drive me mad. I'll lose my mind. How many years did I have to wait for her? A lifetime . . . but she still radiates the same quiet, angelic light. I used to think I would crush her delicacy, but she is generous, and in bed she gives without effort.

When he approached her again, she said, "Please don't mention that business to anybody. I'm afraid of the scandal."

"Scandal?"

"It's enough that people talk about our marriage."

"It's legal, and in accordance with the correct ways of God and His Prophet."

"Of course it is, but this other business—no one will leave us alone."

"I'm not going to do anything."

"So how will you deal with it?"

"I'm only going to humiliate him."

"Oh, have a heart!"

He nearly went back to her to take her in his arms, but it was time for work, and he could not delay the market. He went into the bedroom to change, and stood in front of the dressing table pondering his hair and his moustache. White hairs grew at the sides of his head, undisguised by the dye. That was natural, but since he had finally won her, time ought to have stopped so that he could make up for what had been lost. The love of his life, the first girl in his life. Poverty had kept him from her when he was a lad, helping his father as he stood with the tripod on the sidewalk of Agriculture Street, waiting for the sick cattle that the abattoir would not accept. A farmer would appeal to his father to slaughter an animal already in its death throes.

"Shall we take the knife to it?"

"How much?" The animal's owner would push for the highest price.

"Look, just be grateful we'll take it away as carrion. And may God provide for me and my children."

"Go ahead, then."

Father and son would carry it home, where they would skin it and cut it up. They would send the head, shanks, and offal to a tripe merchant to hawk in the street, and they would sit on the sidewalk the following morning to sell the rest.

She would lean out of her window, shining like the morning sun, her fleshy arms protruding from a light, sleeveless summer garment. He would stare at the window, forgetting himself until his father's voice scolded him. "Are you with me, Osman?"

She continued to develop in front of him, as he observed her femininity in her school pinafore, or a blouse and skirt, or a black silk gallabiya, or with a crepe scarf around her head that showed off the whiteness of her face more than it veiled her, until the day she was taken away by the educated man who deserved her—"the daughter of the educated man for the educated man," they kept telling him to his face. He was just a butcher with nothing to his name, who wore a crooked cap on his head, a belt around his white gallabiya soaked in blood, and leather slippers blackened by blood and dust.

The girl went away to the engineer's house at the end of the town, a fine two-story villa that stood in a garden whose fragrances perpetually wafted in the morning air. Its high walls enclosed broad, towering trees, which in turn hid trees fecund with guavas, mangoes, and limes.

Was she ever aware of him? He could never be sure. He would follow her on her way to school, and on the platform of the train that took her to the provincial capital when she transferred to the higher institute. She responded to his importunities with few words, staring at the ground with an endearing bashfulness.

"Go on, go back. What will people say?"

He would return home sorrowfully, leaving his princess to her affairs, but his heart, alight with its eternal fire, did not cool off. "One day she has to be my wife, whatever happens."

And now here she was behind him, laying his cotton shawl around his shoulders, placing the two ends on the chest of his imposing gallabiya, stroking the back of his neck, and turning him around toward her in order to press a kiss on his moustache.

"For my sake, don't make more of this business than it deserves."

"What do you mean?"

"He's a reckless boy. Think of him as a dumb animal."

"No—he's the smartest person in town. I raised him."

"Just a couple of slaps to his cheeks, in private. Nothing more."

"Leave me to deal with it."

He went out of the room, coughing to dislodge the remnants of yesterday's hashish session, unbolted the door, stamped his feet on the mat, and before leaving the landing asked, "Do you want anything?"

"Just your safe return."

He put out a hand to lean on the banister, as his lungs were awakened by the clean air of the morning and shook him up with a series of violent coughs. The blood rushed to his dark face, making him look like a piece of liver. He spat out the phlegm at the entrance to the building and trod it in with a shiny brown shoe. The smell of manure struck his nose, and the lowing of the cattle behind the walls of the byre facing the building reverberated in his ears. He peered over the broad door to see his men distributing the fodder mixed with rice straw around the long troughs, and the cows greedily munching the food.

How could this dog dare to touch his mistress?

He must be mad, completely mad. The wretch, he doesn't appreciate his blessings, bites the hand that rescued him from hunger. Forgets that I took him in to work with his brother, even though I wasn't comfortable with him. What is a mute doing with us in a butcher's shop? He can certainly set up a goza, the imp, run you a hundred refills in a minute. Squats in front of you like a skinny whelp. Doesn't stop making signs.

She asks me not to punish him, so that what he did doesn't become a scandal! How is that, when I know him better than anyone? And will he refrain from his café prattle? Time was, he'd set up my goza and I'd give him the sign to talk, and he'd come out with somebody's life story, or what somebody else had done. The news of the whole town was in his pocket. He knew what was said behind walls—knew the secrets of the bedroom and what was concealed in people's hearts. That's where his danger lies.

Tell us, ya Houda . . . .

And the storyteller begins . . . .

There's the teacher who seduces the luscious pupil—he brings her close to him through the pretext of marking her exercise book, when all he wants is to get hold of those two little innocents lying in their warm cradle, their mother's milk—as it were—still clinging to the corners of their mouths. This cursed educator swoops down on them, plucking at their young immaculacy.

And the driver who selects an attractive female passenger to sit beside him. He changes gear and in all innocence settles his elbow on the soft, padded mound next to him, and jiggles the steering wheel to keep up the slight but arousing oscillation on her breast, up and down.

And the doctor who practices his profession while lusting for the submissive body. As the patient groans with a pain that runs through her bones, he taps his fingers on the sensitive spots, and feels malevolently between her thighs, while he knows that the origin of the pain is in her molar.

Now I'm going to be one of his stories.

He'll talk about Shams and expose me because I didn't help him to get married when he asked me to. He'll look for revenge, and tell everyone he's having a relationship with her: The maallim sends me to deliver things to her apartment. She's waiting for me in her see-through clothes that reveal the wonders of her body. She says, "Come in, ya Houda." I find the choicest foods laid out on the great dining table that stretches across the hall. I eat till I'm full, then she takes me to a perfumed bathroom and leads me behind the bathtub curtain once she's taken off the few clothes she's wearing, and we stand naked under the water of the shower. She pulls me to her and I devour her firm, red lips. Then I lift her up in my arms to carry her to the soft bed with its glossy pink silk spread. We roll around on it at our leisure, then I go back to consuming the food of all varieties, and she picks me out the best fruits from the basket that's placed among the dishes like a flower vase.

The sun rising behind the houses struck the maallim's face and woke him from his nightmare. Raging, roaring, he tried to loosen his balled fists but could not. He leaned on the fence of the mosque for a time, watching the street wake up, doors and windows being opened, women going out onto the balconies to hang out bedclothes, farmers emerging from the narrow side streets on donkeys and leading cattle that strode resolutely to the fields on the promise of breakfast for their empty stomachs.

That's what the mute's imagination will add, and the people will believe him to spite me. And the dog has never set foot inside my apartment. He stood on the doormat—she told me—and held out the bag of vegetables, which she put down behind the closed half-door. Then he held out the bag of meat—she told me—and she put that behind the half-door too. Then he dusted off his empty palms to ask her, "Do you want anything else?"

"Wait," she said.

She turned her back to him, meaning to give him some money. When she turned around again she found his jaw had dropped down to his chest and his slobber was dribbling uncontrollably down his front. Instead of putting out his hand to take the money, he planted it on her bosom and his fingers grabbed tight hold of one of her breasts.

I saw the marks on it when I took it out of its hiding place that night, and I couldn't go on. I asked her, "Whose fingers are these?"

She wept. I pushed away from her, shaking her naked form forcefully. "Who put his prints here on this place of secrets?"

She turned to the wall to hide her face, and I pulled her roughly. "A black night with no end, this is! Are you playing around, Shams?"

"God forbid, ya maallim!"

"Whose hand got printed on your tit?"

"It was the boy Houda," she said quickly, and without trying to prepare the ground.

"Who!?"

"Houda—the mute."

The bastard! Is this what I brought him up for? With the woman of my house, the dumb cur! Doesn't he know he's invaded my paradise with a horde of red hell's devils? How much of my life and my energies have I spent to win my sweetheart? And in a rabid moment he makes a grab, with no inhibitions, with no thought for the consequences. How long have I toiled and labored? I have no beginning. There is no first step. They were all steps up to climb her high ladder.

My father died. Then came the 1967 war, and army units spread among our towns. I managed to get a small shop on the main street, and a great piece of luck brought me together with the commander of a unit of soldiers that landed on the town. He was into dope, and we met at the house of Abu Ashour, who ran a secret hashish den there for the local worthies. A word here, a word there—he turned out to be a really good sort, and we've remained good friends ever since. I would send him a piece of steak or a shin of lamb, so that he would fall in love with my meat. And I would laugh out loud at his boundless jokes—he didn't care about the government, or even the president.

One evening he said to me, "They've authorized me to find a supplier for the unit. What about helping me out?"

"I'd be more than happy to," I said.

I spoke to the greengrocer next to my shop, and I took on the supply of meat. I entered the magic gates of that propitious time, the six years from the Setback to the Crossing. I accumulated riches without beginning or end. I erected not two apartment buildings but three. I established not one byre but two. I drove a

25

Mercedes. I traveled all over God's broad earth. I acquired an apartment in Alexandria, where I took the wife and children every summer. I put all the children—boys and girls—through school until they got their university degrees. My first wife was a good woman, who lived with me through the lean days with no complaints and supported me with all her energies. I never brought her into the shop—she stayed concealed like a jewel at home, raising the kids. And she was a very good cook.

The fire of Shams continued to burn bright in my heart, never dying, until the day the town was shaken by the terrible accident that killed her husband, when he was hit by a strange car at the edge of town. She wore black for a whole year, which added to her beauty, and the grief suffused her tender soul and made it all the more transparent.

I made bold to present myself, and met with a smooth response. No one in her family objected, and I prepared a wonderful apartment for her in the new building and put it in her name.

That this good-for-nothing could pollute such a treasure with his filthy hand!

Houda was a café boy. I took him on to work for me for nothing but my own amusement, to cheer me up with his antics and his mimicking of all and sundry. I employed him as my monkey—instead of leaving him for everyone, I claimed him entirely for myself.

He used to go around the cafés looking for anyone to send him off to buy hashish, or waiting for someone to call him to prepare the gozas and coals and begin setting up the refills. He preferred the educated men because they tipped better, and because he could store away useful connections he might need later. The educated men in turn preferred him over others because he could deliver two favors: he could make them laugh and get them stoned.

As for the other men, he would sit as one of them, and smoke as one of them, and drink at the expense of one of them. He would call to the café owner and order tea (one hand forming a tumbler, stirred by the index finger of the other) or fenugreek (one hand stretched out flat, as he blew on it) or, if he was really in the mood, a Turkish coffee with sugar (thumb against middle of index finger) or with just a touch of sugar (thumb against tip of index finger).

They would ask him to mimic so-and-so, but he would refuse until they hinted at ten or twenty-five piasters. If he flatly refused he would swipe the air with his hand, purse his lips, and leave with a repeated and decisive clicking of the tongue.

If the hashish was good and had battled and conquered him, he would begin to tell stories in fine form. He knew the troublemakers, the bribetakers, and the illicit relationships—he knew the man who in the heat of the afternoon visited the wife of his friend who was away, and the man who in the dark of the night visited the wife of his friend who was ill. He was quite familiar with the men whose passion it was to sleep with prepubescent girls and boys. He knew the low, godless types who fornicated with jennies and bitches. And he could distinguish the woman who applied kohl to her eyes for her husband from the tart who applied kohl for the young man who spent hours day and night hanging around her house.

And he might get really carried away and talk about politics. Israel was one-eyed Dayan (a hand covering one eye, the other eye staring). The government was a prayer bruise on the forehead, while crossed wrists indicated the iron shackle. And when he referred to the detested secret policeman, he would move his eyeballs right and left, mime abject fear on his face, and shrink his head down into his shoulders.

If there was a stranger among the men he wasn't sure about, he would say that he minded his own business (running one hand across the palm of the other), that he prayed the five daily prayers (putting his hands to the sides of his head five times and screeching *Allahu akbar:* "Abar! . . . Abar!"), that he worked all day for an honest crust (bringing his fingers together at his mouth), and that at the end of the day he accompanied his friends to the café and drank tea, but didn't smoke hashish, except to spice up the honey-tobacco, then went home to bed right after the evening prayer (resting his head on his palm) in order to get up early and pray the dawn prayer communally (throwing his head back, cupping his ears in his hands, and calling, "Abar! . . . Abar!"). And he would point a finger to the heavens to remind the ignorant stranger that there is a great eye, the eye of God, watching our deeds, which are recorded by two angels tied around our necks, who are charged with writing down the bad and the good we do. Thus Houda evaded the pitfall of talking politics with a stranger out to dig holes in the pathways of this rough world. He would bend over the reed of the goza, take a few deep breaths, envelope his head in the cloud of smoke, and shake his hand in the stranger's face to say, "Don't talk about politics, or you'll disappear behind the sun" (pulling his collar up, sinking his head into the neck of his gallabiya, and pointing to the sky).

Is he going to make me one of his stories? I have the right to kill him. Truly. "Protect yourself from the evils of those you've been kind to." My wife is not going to be the talk of the town, mute. I'll teach you.

He entered Agriculture Street and went along greeting the traders who had opened their shops and whose assistants had begun to set up the displays of goods outside the doors on the sidewalk. Wary of the crowds, of which the first waves had started, he kept to the right side of the road to avoid being bumped into by a donkey carrying piles of vegetables coming straight from the fields near the town or from the surrounding villages. Incense was everywhere, and incantations from radios mixed with early morning songs and early morning Quran. Reciters from the town, calling at the shops to chant blessings after their return from the cemetery, squatted on benches holding their large bundles, then went out onto the street fearful that the forenoon sun would climb too high before they finished their daily rounds.

A column of smoke rose obliquely from inside the shop to cloud the maallim's face. He fanned it away with his hand as his coughing started up again, and he said to the boy wielding the censer, "Not too much . . . not too much."

He gave him a ten-piaster coin from his pocket and hit him lightly on the back of the neck. "Get out of here. Go and see to somebody else."

He sat on the high wooden counter, trying to get its drawer to shut properly, when he heard the cry of Shaykh Saadoun al-Hosari: "Hayyyy! Qayyuuum!"

He was overjoyed, the lines on his forehead cleared, and he said to himself in true delight, "The shaykh's back!"

The shaykh came in, his arms wide. "Allah, Allah! Oh, my Beloved Prophet!"

3

A shaykh with no Azhar education, he had no experience of
standing in pulpits, and did not know all the chapters of the
Quran by heart. He also neither led people in prayer nor gave religious pronouncements or judgments. He was just a dervish who
wandered all over and loved mulids and zikrs, but did not belong
to any particular Sufi sect. It was not his inclination to be a member of a group: he was free and unshackled, and went from place
to place and from community to community. He could not bear to
abide long in one land. He feared nothing, but he could not stick
at anything. When the ecstatic state came upon him, he would
quit whatever place he was in without looking back, and without
worrying about leaving work, wife, or children behind—he merely
obeyed the mysterious call, wandered until he stopped at the
appointed place, and stayed there as long as God willed. Then he
would heed the call again and return suddenly, when nobody
expected it.

He worked with his brother, Hagg Radwan al-Hosari, in a large
mat-making shop. Everyone finds their own path in life. Hagg
Radwan was a scrupulous man who wore clean clothes, always pre-
ferring white—the headscarf, the gallabiya, the sandals, the prayer
beads constantly in his hand. The white he loved even flowed over
to his shining, blond visage. His feelings were concealed behind a
sedate self-confidence and a pleasant smile that never left his face,
even in the extreme of anger. He lived with his good-hearted wife

without children, so he made his brother's children his own, bringing them close to him. During the long absences of their father, they became more attached to him and made him their real father. They called him "Aba," even when their original father was around, because they knew he could leave the house, the shop, the whole town at any time and disappear to only God knew where.

Despite all this, Shaykh Saadoun was skilled in his work, cleverly arranging the rushes and the cords to make a floor mat or a prayer mat. He would squat on the wooden frame, letting the nimble fingers of one hand work on their own, passing the rush lightly from cord to cord, while with the other hand pulling the wooden crosspiece to strike the weave, so that the mat was compacted and would hold together. Thus he spent his day until he finished what he had begun.

On other days he would be seen with the apprentices carrying the mats up to the broad open area at the corner of the street and spreading them out in the sun to dry the rushes. The shaykh would lay out mat after mat, bending his back to bunch the rushes tighter together with the cords to make it all firmer, finally tying off the ends of the cords tightly. The mat was then ready for the customer.

He would work determinedly, all the time talking to himself, but at any time the sublimity might come upon him and he would cry out at the top of his voice: "Hayyy! Oh, my Beloved Prophet!" He would throw his turban down and twist left and right on the surface of the mat, turning his face to the sun, clapping palm against palm in an ecstasy of which nobody but he knew the cause. "Allah, Allah! Ya Abu Khalil!"

From this, people would know that his journey this time would not be a long one, because one need go no farther than Zagazig to reach the mulid of Abu Khalil, the most famous of that town's saints. Or perhaps he would cry as he kicked his legs in the air:

"Allah, Allah! Ya Qinawi!" In which case he would be traveling to Qina. Or he might call on Disouqi, which meant he would be going north to Disouq.

These were the conclusions people came to, but perhaps they were wrong. A mulid, even the longest, would never last more than a week or two, and if it were far away it might need up to a month to travel there and back, but the shaykh was absent for many months. Sometimes he disappeared for a whole year, or two years. Once he was away for nearly six.

Maallim Osman looked forward to his surprise appearances, which filled him with joy. Now he would have company in his long nights, and someone to talk to in the work day. Also, the shaykh never came to see him empty-handed. He leaned close and whispered, so that the maallim's men would not catch what they were saying, "I've brought you—for the love of God's Prophet—a mix that will make the pious man forget his prayers!"

And he reached into the pocket of his striped Upper Egyptian gallabiya and pulled out the package wrapped in thick paper, putting it under the maallim's nose. "Smell it, and bless the Beloved One."

A tumult was set off in the maallim's head to stir the most tranquil blood. "Allah! Allah, ya mawlana!"

"This, with a blessing on the Dear One, you grind after the evening prayer, and leave it till you're ready to perform. Exactly an hour—before—don't take it on an empty stomach. Then go to it!"

"What will you have to drink, ya mawlana?"

"Coffee with sugar, bless the Prophet!"

The maallim signaled to a boy crouched in a corner carving meat off the bone. "Tell them two coffees with sugar."

When the boy returned with the tray, the shaykh bit onto a dark brown lump. He then held it between his fingers and used a matchstick to pick off a piece of it, which he dissolved at the bottom of the cup after removing the froth on the coffee.

"Pull yourself together, man. You don't look right today."

"Something's bothering me, ya mawlana, but it's a long story."

"All difficulties are as nothing by His command."

"I don't know what to do. Or where to start telling you about it."

"Get it off your chest."

"The boy Houda the mute violated my house!"

"Lord protect us!"

"The filthy wretch! By God, I'll see to him!"

He related what Shams had told him. The shaykh put his arm across his shoulder. "*Say: I seek refuge in the Lord of the daybreak from the evil of that which He created . . . . Say: I seek refuge in the Lord of mankind, the King of mankind, the God of mankind . . . .*"

He had barely finished reciting the two prayers of refuge when he heard the clatter of the wheels outside. The cart stopped precisely in front of the door, and the men came up to carry the carcass to the hooks hanging from the ceiling. The meat was still hot, and blood dripped onto the clean, white tiles.

Houda came in making a big fuss when he saw the shaykh. He bent down to embrace him, kissed his beard, and pointed to the ceiling of the shop. "Ab . . . ab"—God keep you!

The shaykh gave him a friendly smile, and patted him on the shoulder in blessing. Then he pulled him over to the maallim, but although Houda turned to greet him, the maallim did not let him, pretending to be busy giving out orders. Houda backed away, not knowing why the gloomy expression had suddenly come over his boss's face, though he understood what this would mean: he would spend a grouchy day at work. This was how it was with the maallim's temper, which would flare for no reason and dissipate for equally no reason. On the days when he was happy, he was content with Houda and never stopped joking with him. He would send him on one errand after another, and Houda never tired—he would respond eagerly, and immediately do whatever the maallim asked him to.

He wanted to get out of the shop. The shaykh came to his rescue by grasping his hand and signaling that he wanted to have a word with him about an important matter. He took him off to one side, where they were concealed between two cuts of a carcass suspended at the shop front. The shaykh told him that the maallim had that morning broached the question of Houda's marriage. Houda's face lit up.

"And I for my part convinced him that you work well for him and that you have now reached the age when you should be sharing a house with a wife." He had secured the maallim's agreement, and the wedding would take place this week. He hit him playfully on the belly. "There—be happy. You'd better not let us down!"

Houda understood all the signs, but the lump would not leave his throat—the maallim's face did not spell good will, and how could a topic he had been pestering the maallim over for years be resolved in a second? How could the shaykh appear so happy telling him the news, while the maallim ignored him and didn't return his greeting as on other mornings?

Which signs should he believe? Was there some kind of catch?

He let the shaykh know his doubts, signaling to him with tense fingers, "But the look on the maallim's face contradicts what you just said."

"He's preoccupied with something that has nothing to do with you," the shaykh replied.

Houda signed again. "Who will the bride be? Do I know her?"

The shaykh signed back, "Don't you trust your boss to choose a bride for you? She'll be from a good family."

The last question: "Will he help me with the expenses?"

"It won't cost you a millieme," the shaykh reassured him. Then he pushed him gently, to tell him, "Stop asking questions and get back to work, or else he might change his mind. You have to prove to him that you're worthy of being one of his faithful men."

He went back to sit beside his friend, who was intent on the boiling blood that was rising in his veins. But the blend of coffee and opium, as it spread joy through his arteries, lit up his face and warmed his extremities, and his rage subsided. He bent toward the shaykh to ask, "What did you say to him?"

"I told him we'd arranged for him to be married."

"What? Instead of punishing him we're rewarding him?"

"For the Prophet's sake, leave this to me. All you have to do is pay the money and watch."

"Whatever you say."

He leaned back to rest his head against the wall, keeping an eye on his men. Some of them came to stand at the marble counter, some continued to slice the fat and gristle off the red meat, and others rearranged the livers in the illuminated glass-fronted refrigerator. He also observed the arrival of the customers, as the morning sun rose higher and persistently attempted to push through the door and stretch out on the floor embellished with drops of blood.

4

Maallim Osman spoke with you, ya Houda, and it was as if he were striking a taut string eager to be played. He leaned toward Shaykh Saadoun and scanned the men working around him, winking at them. "Isn't that right, men?"

"It's all from the goodness of your heart," they said in one breath.

You leaped to kiss the maallim's hand, which he submitted to the proffered lips, saying piously, "God forbid!"

He asked you through signs to "show us how hard you can work between now and when I settle everything."

Your flame was ignited, ya Houda, and its white-hot fire almost burned you. You kept coming and going, taking off and landing, lifting up and putting down, all with your eye on the maallim—Do you see me?

Before you left the shop, you asked him about the anticipated bride. He drew together the fingers of one hand to indicate patience. "You'll see her on your wedding night." He slapped you playfully on the back of the neck. "And you'll deflower her."

You nodded your head in joy.

"Or don't you trust your maallim, ya Houda?"

"God forbid," you said, pointing to heaven. "The Lord knows."

You were satisfied with what your boss had said. "Let's wait until Thursday," you told yourself. "We're nearly there."

Zaki signaled to you to take the implements and go back to the room to prepare the cart for tonight. He would meet you later once he had acquired the liver left over at the shop. You picked up the tools in a cloth bag, put the small tub under your arm, and tied the carving knives around your waist.

The setting sun shone weak and yellow on the sides of the higher houses, and the crowds of Agriculture Street had almost completely disappeared. The traders who came to the town on market day had gone home, packing up their goods on Datsun pick-up trucks, while the town's own traders had begun to clear their things away on donkey-carts. Vegetable scraps were scattered on the ground, awaiting the council tractor, trodden in by people's feet and mixed with the mud of the street. Goats roamed everywhere, browsing for the scraps. They wandered in a flock, invading the sidewalks and the open shops until somebody chased them away, when they skipped lightly off to whatever they might find next in their path.

You mounted the raised sidewalk to avoid pressing through the flock, and the smell of salted fish assailed your nostrils, so you turned to your left to greet Disouqi the salted fish merchant. Disouqi waved to you more cheerfully than usual and raised his hand to his turban to tell you, "Congratulations!"

"How did you know?" you signed back.

Disouqi replied with a sign to assert that the whole street knew. Then he brought the bunched fingers of both hands to his chest and kissed them with his lips to say, "She's very beautiful."

You were amazed, and tossed your hands in the air.

—Did the maallim announce the news? Or did his apprentices spread the word, so that every seller, trader, and customer knows? The maallim is a good man, he's happy for me, so he wants to invite everybody. The strange thing is that everyone knows who the bride is, and they all give the same hand signs.

You stepped down from the sidewalk to cross to the other side of the street, where you met the owner of the bakery, who signaled to you in the same way as the salted fish merchant had done. You passed by the fruit dealer, who repeated the same sign. You were obliged to respond to them, and you revealed your happiness to all.

—I'm not just a lowly butcher's apprentice who nobody takes any notice of. On the contrary, everybody is celebrating on my behalf, as though I were the only bachelor in this town.

—Shall I continue along the street, calling in to see the fish griller, the aluminum vessel dealer, the potter, the newspaper seller? Or should I take a short cut and go up the steps to the railway station to walk along the platform on my own? Enough of this jollity, let's avoid people until it's time to invite them to the wedding.

You began to climb the station steps. When you reached the paved platform, the stationmaster, sitting in the shade of the ancient English building, caught sight of you. "Congratulations, ya Houda."

He raised his hand high to wave it above his combed-over hair, and came over to you to shake your hand. He pointed to his eyes to announce that he was very happy, and followed that by raising his hands to his chest then kissing them with his lips.

You thanked him and walked among the group of passengers standing under the wooden shelter waiting for the 5:30 train. Walking along the platform in the direction of the iron crossing gates, you spotted the train coming from the south, stirring up the dust at the entrance to the town.

You have never heard the whistle, nor has the clanging of the bell that warns of the closing of the gates ever reached your ears. You judge distances by what your eyes see, not by what your ears hear.

You looked behind you to make sure of the train coming from the other direction and saw it slowly entering the siding, its serpentine body twisting in response to the iron rails. Judging that you had time to cross to the other side, you ducked under the lowered gate and headed in the direction of Mitwalli's café. Adenoidal Aziza was moving among the chairs, spraying water on the ground to settle the dust stirred up by the speeding cars. You signaled to her that you were leaving your tools here until you came back later after taking a bath. "Why have a bath now?" she signed to you. "Wait until your wedding day—it's coming very soon!"

You smiled at her and asked her, "How did you know?"

She tipped the rest of the water out onto the ground, and said, "Everyone knows."

She brought her hands up to her chest, but you stopped her from completing the gesture, saying, "Everyone says she's very beautiful, but I haven't seen her yet."

She pulled her dress up high, bunched it around her buttocks, and walked seductively in front of you—"But she's not as beautiful as me."

You spat outside the café, then trod it in as you left for the main street busy with cars. After a short while you dropped down to the long side street. Now the sun was behind you, throwing an exaggeratedly long shadow in front of you. It raced you, rising and falling, climbing the stones in the road and flowing with the puddles of slop water in your path, stretching and contracting according to your movements as you walked, appearing and disappearing if the shadow of a tall building fell on it. When you neared the cheese factory, you greeted the owner, sitting on a chair in front of the door waiting for the women to come with the evening milking.

It's your fate to see them come out twice, ya Houda. You work the whole day between two milkings. You start your day at dawn and end it with the sunset call to prayer. Not only that, you can't rest yet. You have to wash yourself quickly, then go out to the liver cart to begin the evening's work. Toil and exertion, continuous labor—no rest for you until you are embraced by the darkness of your tomb.

39

Perhaps if you were married you would leave your brother and make do with the work in the shop, to find the time to spend with your wife, to play with her, to have fun with her, to steal a kiss, to hold her tight in a long embrace, to make up for an age of deprivation. Well, let her come, and then we'll see what will happen. You'll give her times of pleasure, and take delight in her all her life, so that she doesn't look at anybody else. She will have eyes only for you, her unrivaled stallion. She will not turn her face to left or right—as if you would give her the chance!

You saw the women neighbors gathered in the shadow of the wall of the big house, the thick, shady mulberry branches bending high over them. They beckoned you, so you approached hesitantly. These crones will start prattling, asking you questions, but you will foil them, because they are just a bunch of wagging tongues, efficiently broadcasting news to every quarter. They are always so scathing of everybody, and nothing impresses them.

You noticed Fakiha among them, in her light summer dress.

—This woman tortures me. Oh, if my bride is as beautiful as her I'll never miss a prayer—I'll perform all five daily, even pray the dawn prayer on time, and I'll prostrate myself to God morning and night.

Her breasts gleamed in the last rays of the sun. Your jaw dropped and you were aware of your drool dribbling uncontrollably. But the killer was not satisfied with that: she threw up her arms, revealing her depilated armpits, to untie her colored headscarf so that her dark hair spilled down her back and hid her earrings. She gathered her hair in a large bun, secured it skillfully from behind, and replaced the scarf, expertly tying up its two ends but leaving a glossy lock to hang over her forehead. And she surprised you with a wink.

Your erection began to rise, but you tried to control yourself, gnashing your teeth. It subsided of its own accord when you

40

shifted your gaze to the other women and in particular to Umm Ali, the owner of the house, her skinny bones wrapped in a tattered old piece of muslin. She was watching you with a vigilant but damp eye, whose moisture ran down the wrinkles of her face. Dark hairs stood out on her lips and chin. Squatting next to her was the wife of Abu Sinna, with her solid, strong build, her vulgar glances, and her marketplace comments. The women smiled and whispered with her. She was a woman who had experienced life, had been around every market there was, and knew the good from the bad. She was a skilled trader of fish, and always argumentative. She never allowed a woman to put her hand near the fish in the basket—she would let out a snort, and yell in the woman's face, "Get your hand away or I'll cut it off!" And if the customer objected to her tone of voice, she would fly in her face: "Get out of here, you whore, or you'll regret it!"

She didn't care whether she sold or not. She had a regular customer who would always buy from her, and she reserved her goods for him. As he headed toward her through the market throng, she would welcome him with genuine warmth. "Bless the Prophet, what a fine day!" By the time he stood before her at her stand she would already have wrapped the required amount, without having to weigh it, her hands through experience being as good as any scales. "Here's your order." And when he put out his hand to pay, she would push it away firmly. "No, please keep it."

Her daughter had taken on her mother's great stature. Emplaced firmly on her substantial thighs, her chin resting on her hand, she was observing you. She smiled at you, but you avoided looking at her and felt momentarily nauseous. The girl was damp down below.

—I'll bet my arm, if she stands up we'll find she's been sitting in a puddle. Am I blind and can't see that? How nice to marry a woman who hangs out her wet drawers on the bedstead every morning. Am I to clean up after her, or after our children? I'm well rid of her and her mother. Thank God the maallim saved me with a solid marriage, and it won't cost me a thing.

"Congratulations, ya Houda," they all said.

You brought your hands up to your head, bowing slightly in modest humility, and signed to them with both hands in supplication that their daughters might find decent men to marry and be safe in their homes.

Usually, the closer you approach, the more they laugh and tease you. You begin to flirt with them—a wink here, a pinch of the waist there, a subtle move to touch a breast. Then you go on to mimic how their husbands walk or how they smoke their gozas, or to list—through sign language—some of their secrets, or to tell them all about someone else who isn't there at the time. When you're not on an errand or busy, you sit with them around a basket of grain picking grit out of it or helping them pluck the mulukhiya or mallow leaves. You lift up any one of the toddlers playing among them or the suckling infants cradled on their mothers' laps and bite him or tickle his sides, not letting him go until he cries, not out of malice—God forbid—but because your fun-making is cruel and rough, and your fingers that you dig into their soft flesh are thin and stiff. Returning a baby to its worried mother you are not averse to pressing the back of your hand into her large, full breasts.

Today there was no time for this play, your head busy with a thousand concerns.

"They're marrying you off, ya Houda!" they said.

So you sat with them for a while, telling them what had transpired between you and Maallim Osman. "The maallim"—you twisted your moustache, puffed up your face, made a large belly—"is going to marry me off"—you drew an imaginary ring on your ring finger, stuck your two index fingers together, then formed a woman's breasts on your chest. "It's going to be on Thursday"—

you stressed this three times with your fingers—"and my bride is as beautiful as the moon"—you kissed your bunched fingers and pointed to the sky. Then you asked them to come to the wedding and dance and make the traditional cries of joy—you placed your hand flat above your mouth and worked your tongue in a long, drawn-out trill.

They asked you to tell them what you would do with your future bride: you hugged the air tenderly and looked fierily toward Fakiha, you closed your eyes and puckered your lips to plant sweet and yearning kisses on your hand and shoulders.

Fakiha signed to you that your bride would play around behind your back. You started shouting at an invisible person nobody but you could see. "Brrrrh! Brrrrh!" They struck their chests and dissolved in laughter, which they eventually recovered from to say, "God damn you, mute!"

You left them in a rage, punching your hands in all directions, turning around to them angrily, then looking in front of you again so as not to lose your balance on the uneven road surface, and you spat over your shoulder before going in the door of the house. In the long passageway you came across blind Aida with an earthenware drum under her arm, beating it skillfully for her younger, blind sister to dance to. The dancer had tied an old piece of cloth around her waist that she had pulled off the head of her middle sister Nawal, who was engrossed in clapping to the rhythm of the drum.

You were astonished at these constantly cheerful blind women, for whom nothing muddied the clarity of their lives, and whose concerns were limited to visits to the cemetery and making the rounds of the houses to recite incantations.

The time for marrying had passed Aida by, and she had grown old. Thick hairs grew from her cheeks, her front teeth protruded from her mouth along with bloody, red gums. She was resigned to her fate, and satisfied herself with having learned by heart some

43

short chapters of the Quran and a few songs to be sung among the women at wedding celebrations. When she was invited to sing at a wedding she would receive her due and return home, happy with the money she had collected and with the container her sister carried, overflowing with wedding food. She would give the money to her mother, and they would all sit around the food together, raising it to their ravenous mouths, then go to sleep in a joy unequaled anywhere in the world.

Meanwhile, you were angry at your lot, not satisfied with what God had decreed for you. You wanted to possess a house completely your own, not to share a rented room with your brother, a situation that had lasted a long time and that even that morning had seemed as though it would never end.

—Praise God for inspiring the maallim to choose a bride for me and a new house. He's taken responsibility for me, and I won't spend a millieme. I certainly deserve the best—I've spent my life with him, serving him in great and small. It's right that he should reward me, I'm his man.

You turned slightly toward the door to make room for the Azhar student, who had secured the lock on his room and was going out, leaning on his bad leg, pressing on it with his hand and pulling the other leg behind him, stirring up a light cloud of dust. He was all wet, dripping ablution water from his hair and his fingers. The scent of musk from his clean, white gallabiya caught your nostrils. He supported himself against the wall with his arm and signed to greet you. You mumbled, "Ab . . . ab," and wished him well, and you asked him not to forget you in his prayers.

Then he surprised you, because you thought that—being a stranger and having nothing to do with anyone, attending the institute and returning to spend the day crouched over his books in the dark of his room, being seen only when going to the mosque and coming back from the mosque—he would be the last to know.

44

He signed, "May the same come true for your first son."

"Ab . . . ab."

The lock opened in your hand and you pulled it free of the clasp. You plunged into the dark, looking for the things you needed in order to take a bath and scrub your skin clean of the accumulated filthy layers of animal blood mixed with the sweat of running around and the sweat of sleeping in a room that God's living sun never entered.

You stood naked in the broad, shallow tub, having filled your left hand with soap suds, and picked up your resting member to massage it gently, arousing its suppressed longing. You closed your eyes and conjured up the market women, putting together a perfect woman from the body parts you had packed away in your mind, as you did every day.

Fakiha always won out over the others, erasing them from your imagination to take the leading role in the scene. In her stupefying nakedness, she became all women, not one woman. Then the scene that you saw one night began to take shape, and there was no stopping it. The hashish had swept your head away, and you returned from your evening out completely stoned. When you reached the main door, something inside you urged you to peer through the gaps in the tall wooden window by the entrance. You saw Fikri squeezed between the two mountains of her mighty thighs, as she gave and took from him in small movements. Her excitement gradually rose. Her face, contorted with pleasure, turned to the pillow, scattering her sweaty tresses. You forgot yourself, ya Houda, and thrust the whole of your face between the two wings of the window, which had opened up against the wall, and you were so engrossed in watching, you didn't notice that your head had passed between two of the iron bars. When the couple reached their impassioned climax you responded with them and shrieked at the top of your voice.

Fikri looked around at you over his shoulder, and, still naked, got up slowly and surely. You tried to extract your head but the iron bars held it mercilessly tight, as if they had stretched for a moment to let you through then become solid once more.

Fakiha, who had jumped up terrified, wrapped herself in the bedclothes snarling, cursing, and gesticulating. You were still occupied in freeing yourself when Fikri came at you from behind, raining blows on your backside with the sole of a shoe heavy with the dirt of the filthy street. You could not scream, or you would have woken the neighbors and alerted your sleeping brother in the next room to what you had done. You accepted the pain in silence until Fikri was able to bend the iron bars apart and pull your head out to shove you roughly against the wall. Your head was spinning and you fell to the floor. You didn't realize you had been asleep until you heard the voice of Blind Amin from the minaret of the market mosque.

Today, you decided to save your fluid until your wedding night, to preserve it in its vigor rather than squandering it. You bent down to the tub and poured the lukewarm water over your body, which you scrubbed thoroughly with the loofah.

Then you got out of the tub, dried yourself under your arms and between your legs on a tattered towel, and put on your clean gallabiya. You spent some time scrutinizing your dry face in the remains of the mirror embedded in the mud wall, and dabbed on a few drops of scent from a small bottle that lay among some folded clothes.

After the sunset call to prayer you leave your room, your hair coiffed, and trot along in your gallabiya, pushing the cart in front of you. You don't talk to the women as you pass by their circle, and take no notice of their signs. You are serious and stern now, on your way to the company of men, whom you will invite to join in the all-night wedding celebrations.

And there at Mitwalli's café you might meet an educated man who will send you to the hashish dealer—if you see that he is worth the long trip, you will agree—and you will not object to preparing the goza and the coals, to setting things up, perhaps even smoking a couple yourself until Zaki comes. Then you will light the burner, and once the flame is clear and steady you will put it under the broad frying pan and pour the oil in, while Zaki spreads out the liver behind the glass of the cart, cuts it into small pieces on a thick wooden chopping block, coats it in the coarse bran, and tosses it into the pan for you to keep an eye on with the long-handled skimmer.

You wash the tomatoes and vegetables well under the café tap and prepare a spicy salad. Meanwhile, Zaki has fetched the fresh bread from the bakery and spread it out on top of the cart to dry a little. When a customer comes, he folds a flat of bread to make a sandwich, filling it with pieces of liver, once he has weighed them, and sprinkling parsley and chopped salad on it. Every now and then he gives you a shove to call the customer, and you screech at the top of your voice, "Beek . . . beek!"

There is no relation between your shout and your wares, but your customer—whether a café regular, or one of the lads from the service taxi station, or a stranger passing through the town on a long night journey—knows what you mean, and they like your call, and your desperate attempts to announce the food. Perhaps some even come specially, not for the sake of the sandwich, but for the chance to joke around with you and tease, provoke, and rile you, not leaving you alone until you threaten them with the skimmer, and a broken skull. It may even end up with you leaving the stand and chasing after them, putting your hand to your neck to say, "I'll slit your throat if I catch you!"

5

Shaykh Saadoun performed the evening prayer in the big mosque, then slipped away from the other worshipers surreptitiously so that his brother Hagg Radwan would not ask where he was going. The hagg was reciting some short chapters of the Quran, which he would follow with the nightfall supplications, the long, colored prayer-string of ninety-nine beads never leaving his hand.

He did not head for his house, across the street from the mosque, but instead made his way down the slope to the market district.

—The children don't need me to spend the evening with them, or even to be there at all. They flock around their uncle Radwan and treat him as a father. They celebrate for a while when I return home to them unexpectedly, but how quickly they lose interest. None of them will sleep in my arms. Their uncle's house is their home, and they call in at my room like strangers. My wife doesn't expect much from me, and makes no demands on me. She lives in the house not because she likes it or has any affection for me, but to be close—she says—to the children. Besides, she has nowhere else to go.

A cooling off, emotional indigestion, a shared life loathed. Not overnight, but in stages. The end came when he complained of his impotence with her to his friends at Abu Ashour's hashish den. One of them burst out, "I have just the cure for you."

"Put me out of my misery, may God not afflict you."

"You'll have it tomorrow. And say a special prayer for me."

"I'll pray that you visit the Prophet's tomb, God willing."

The next night, he ordered a round from Abu Ashour, and swore that not one of them would touch his own hashish. "It's my treat."

He waited for the friend with the cure, who arrived late. They made room for him in the circle, and when Qunsul passed the reed to the shaykh's mouth he held it out pleasantly to his friend, looking him directly in the eye. "Felicitations, Osta."

The osta, the bicycle repairman, sucked until the coals sparked and popped and danced on the tobacco bowl. He drew a deep breath that stirred the bowels of the goza, and the water spilled out over his mouth, as pure white fire burned and finished off the tobacco and the hashish, leaving nothing behind.

"Well done. You're a champion." The shaykh clapped his hands. Abu Ashour swayed on his seat behind the sand box, and stroked his long, flowing, moustacheless beard.

"My Beloved Prophet!"

The osta spent the whole evening without giving any indication that he had brought the cure for the shaykh, waiting until they went out into the dark street before pulling him to one side and holding out his hand with a small pot. "Before you go near the wife don't drink any water, though you can have a light bite of something. When you want to get an erection, take some of this on your finger and rub it all over."

"From top to bottom?"

"Of course—are we going to get one bit standing and leave the rest?"

"So it's not going to abandon me halfway through and go to sleep?"

"By the grace of God, like iron till the morning."

He did as the man advised. Shortly after he had inserted himself, though, he suddenly felt spent and wanted to withdraw, but was unable to. He pulled his body away from his wife in vain—he remained hooked up down there, as though a djinn were hanging onto him from inside and did not want to set him free.

He tried once, twice, and again and again.

Sweat flowed copiously over the two naked bodies. He put his hand down below to pull, but nothing moved from its place. She tried to lift him off with her arms, with no result. He called out, "Brother Hagg Radwan!"

His voice rang out in the night silence, a cry for help, with no response.

"Help, anyone! Help me, Hagg Radwan!

His brother burst into the room. As his eyes took in the scene, he reversed to push his wife and the children away, then went back in alone and locked the door. He extinguished the lamp and approached the bed. The shaykh was tugging at himself, and shouting, "Help me, you dimwit!"

He pushed with his forearms at the sides, trying to lift his rear. Hagg Radwan picked up the water pot from its stand near the bed and splashed water on the area where they were stuck. The shaykh fell on his side, panting, while the woman disappeared under the covers, crying bitterly.

Hagg Radwan went out, clapping one hand on the other in disbelief. "God damn you . . . God damn you!"

The shaykh stopped going to Abu Ashour's hashish den. When he met the bicycle repairman in the street and he asked about the cure, he lied to avoid becoming the talk of the town. "Just great." And he had to restrain himself from falling on the man's neck and squeezing so hard that his head came away from his body.

"Peace and the mercy of God and His blessings on you."

"Where are you off to?"

"Just something I have to see to."

"Shall we expect you?"

"Yes." And he gave the same reply to any of his friends from the den who asked.

He leaned backward to compensate for the steepness of the street, in the treacherous dark. When he approached a street lamp and the boys who were gathered in its circle, they left their games and ran to him in high spirits, surrounding him and grasping the edges of his quftan, clinging on to his sleeves, and pulling on both ends of the silk shawl that fell over his chest. "Shaykh Saadoun, give us your blessing."

He took a small bottle of musk from the depths of his great pocket and sprinkled it on them. They stretched out their hands, and he dispensed light drops of the liquid into their open palms, which they raised to their faces or wiped on their gallabiyas. But this was not enough—they followed him until he took out a handful of peanuts and threw them in the air above their heads for them to snatch in their hands or scrabble for in the dust of the street.

"Give us your blessing."

He took some caramel drops coated in flour from his other pocket and scattered them over the children—their shouts multiplied and they swarmed for the sweet balls. He left them searching for the drops swallowed up by the dust and moved on to another circle, at another street lamp.

A walk that would normally take him a quarter of an hour took him two hours, because he could not get away from the children. He loved children, and they returned the love. They were anointed by him, and they breathed in the smell that wafted from his perpetually clean clothes.

These innocents did not know his goal. They did not know the plan he was concocting in his head. He was aware of this

51

alarming contradiction between his pure relationship with these children and what he was secretly planning on behalf of the maallim, his lifelong friend. At least, he would not be doing anything to offend God: the mute had done wrong, there was no doubt, and he deserved to be punished.

—Everybody knows our plan, and the whole town supports us, everyone for his own reasons. And I can never forget what he did to me personally. Long years may have passed, but every time I remember it a fire ignites in my nether parts.

One burning hot summer afternoon, Shaykh Saadoun was bent over a mat, fixing its rushes in place, tightening its cords, in the broad open area near the shop. His calico-panted rump was high in the air, his whole weight leaning on his forearms as his hands worked busily, and his head wrapped in his bright white turban was sunk between his shoulders. He saw only the blank mat and its long lines of rushes, which he pulled together tightly to make it strong and long lasting.

Suddenly, somebody sent a stone flying that collided with his dangling testicles from behind. He fell flat on his stomach, in enormous pain, and let out a groan that set the houses of the neighborhood quaking, then began rolling from side to side with his legs in the air as he held on to what was between them with both hands. The pain was more than a mule might have borne, and he screamed, "God's burning fire! God's burning fire!"

That was all he said before he fainted. He came to in a white hospital room. He stood dizzily, concerned with nothing but knowing who threw the stone.

"It doesn't matter," they said. "Praise God you're all right."

"I won't rest until I know who it was."

"What good will it do?"

"I'll take my revenge on him, and his family."

"Well—the Lord already took revenge by tying up his tongue, and he has no family."

"The mute!"

The very one. It's an old feud, you piece of dirt, but time hasn't wiped it out.

There he was, standing behind the cart, under the neon light, beside his brother, turning the liver with the skimmer, filling the great street with his cries: "Beek . . . beek!"

The screeching was drowned out by the sound of the signal bell announcing the departure of the nine o'clock train. The shaykh crossed the track before the gate closed, passing through the vehicles and animals that were held up on both sides. He looked right and left to cross the asphalt road, and now he was in the spot that was alive with the lights of the fruit stand and the bright white bilela cart, appetizing steam rising from its containers. The shaykh's mouth watered, but he knew he did not have time to enjoy a dish of bilela with cream and nuts.

The patrons of Mitwalli's café called out to him, "Come and join us, ya mawlana."

"God grant you His blessings, no thank you."

"A quick smoke."

"I've given it up, by God. Zaki, may I have a word?"

Zaki left what he was doing and walked out of the light of the neon lamp to go to the shaykh, who leaned forward to warn him, "You'd better not have felt sorry for him and tipped him off."

"Of course not, ya mawlana. It's the maallim's orders."

"It's to your benefit, so that he calms down and learns what's right."

Houda watched them talk as he stirred the liver, but he could not understand anything, as it was too dark to make out the movement of their lips. He could read lips by watching them carefully, and knew if he was being insulted or if what was being said had nothing to do with him. He rested the skimmer on the side of the pan and joined them. He asked the shaykh through signs, "Is the maallim going to keep his promise?"

"Are we playing around?" the shaykh signed back, "Of course he is!"

Houda stretched out his snout to kiss the shaykh's shoulder, and raised his hands to the heavens. "Ab . . . ab!" Then he signed to him, "It's all thanks to you. But how will it happen when I don't have a room to myself, or the furniture to set up a new house, or suitable clothes for the wedding?"

"The maallim will take care of all that," the shaykh signed, "and I myself will carry out whatever he says. You will have a house and furniture."

Houda brought his hands to the sides of his face—"Ab . . . ab"—to thank the shaykh for his efforts, but his heart was still perturbed, and he asked again, "Will I have a proper wedding, with singing girls and dancers? And have you arranged for the marriage official to come?"

He asked the shaykh to forgive him for his many questions, because the whole town knew about the wedding, and he wanted to be sure it was really happening. The shaykh patted him on the stomach. "Put a summer melon in your belly, as they say—don't worry about a thing. Everything's taken care of."

"Ab . . . ab." Still he asked, submissively, "Who is the bride? Everyone knows except me."

"It's a surprise," signed the shaykh, "and when you see her on your wedding night you'll thank me, because it was me—yes, me—who chose her for you. All you need to know is that she is one of the most beautiful girls in town."

He went back to work reassured, the joy on his face beaming in the neon and adding to its light. He turned up the flame of the burner under the pan, tossed some liver into the hot oil, and called out in a warbling voice, "Beek . . . beek."

The shaykh once again warned Zaki, who felt powerless under the threat. "You'll lose your living. Yes, he's your brother, but you only have one life."

Then he pushed him back to the cart to carry on with his work. "God grant you his blessings."

He went down again to the narrow Market Street, leaning backward to avoid a sudden tumble. He gathered up the ends of his gleaming quftan and pushed at an ancient door, which responded grudgingly. He entered sideways, scraping his belly on the closed wing of the door, and clapped his hands. "Anybody here?"

The entrance hall was totally dark, so he felt his way along the narrow walls until he stood in the light of the dim lamp that hung from the ceiling. Here he perceived bodies moving and heard muffled mutterings, but still he could not see clearly. He heard a woman's voice from deep inside the room. "Who's that? Shaykh Saadoun?"

Then all around, there was a general shout of "Welcome, ya mawlana!"

"How are you, ya Farha?"

"As you see—just as you left me."

The smell of the matured bouza met his nostrils. Farha wiped her hands on an old rag and welcomed him with arms outstretched. The shaykh picked her up off the straw-scattered floor and gazed into her living eye, ignoring the fixed stare of her glass one. He kissed her on the cheeks, the hair of his beard grazing the end of her nose.

"You're still pretty, girl."

"And you're still fit and strong, God bless the Prophet."

"That was in the old days."

He kept her thin body suspended up on the mound of his belly until he became aware of the wraithlike beings spread about on the straw. Some of them staggered to their feet, holding each other up, to exclaim, to applaud, or to whistle with their crooked mouths.

55

"What a fuss!"

"Why does the shaykh get this treatment? We're here with you every day."

"Her sweetheart."

"Sit down, you fleabags, all of you."

They all sat down at once, and tugged at the tail of the shaykh's quftan. "Sit with us."

"All right."

"Forget about them and come with me." She led him by the hand to the table stacked with the empty mugs, and went into the dark behind the stand to fetch him a stool of plaited palm leaves, onto which, after gathering up his tails, the shaykh lowered his awesome posterior. Farha scooped a large mugful from the barrel for him and placed it on the thick plastic tablecloth, then she spread out some sheets of newspaper and laid out two grilled fish and some spring onions. "Enjoy!"

"Not one of them has changed," he said, pointing to her customers, who were engrossed in clamorous conversation. There was Farouk the blacksmith, Faris the waterwheelwright, Abduh the barber, Abu Neama the gallabiya tailor—all masters of trades worn down by the passage of time. No one needed their services any more, but they insisted on keeping their ancient shops open. They would wake at the crack of dawn and go to Market Street to hoist up the iron shutters on their shop doors, then they would sit on their wooden benches held together with coarse nails.

Farouk would neither light his furnace nor pump the bellows, but would wait patiently for someone from one of the neighboring villages to come to have a sickle honed or to order a new mattock head, or a worker from the only mill in the town to sharpen the chisels they used to roughen the grooves in the millstones.

As for Faris, his trade had become completely extinct with the spread of motorized irrigation pumps. The most he could expect was when somebody called on him to remove the skeleton of an old waterwheel. Once, his saw never rested from cutting the teeth of the wooden cogs, large and small. Perhaps it might occur to someone as a favor to have a low table made, and he would be obliged to make it. But this was nothing compared to what he used to do.

Abduh—who used to go around with his leather bag to the farmers in their fields and the rich people in their homes, and at the end of the season collect his dues in vegetables—was now universally neglected. Everyone went to the new salons, which gulled them with their mirrors stuck to every wall. The fancy boys wanted hairstyles he did not know how to do, and he became an object of mockery, as they made fun of his profession and his traditional, old-fashioned appearance.

The same had happened to Abu Neama: his trade had been swept away by factory-made clothes. Nobody today looked for kashmir or a fine piece of English wool, or liked to order the tailoring of a broadcloth cloak or a shiny, silk-fronted, buttoned waistcoat. Shops and businesses specializing in imported clothes became common. Was he supposed to wait for somebody to come to him each season with a piece of cloth he had received as a gift from a worker returning from an oil state and ask for unheard of styles?

They all spent their day sitting in front of their shops until the sunset call to prayer, when they returned home with their meager takings, having agreed to meet later at Farha's bouza shop.

They would come together in a circle, cursing the treacherous times and recalling the bygone days of their glory, casting suspicious glances at every stranger, determined that no one else should join their group. They made do with their own company, and this night venue was their only breathing space, an intimate meeting place without substitute.

"Count them."

"One, two, three, four . . . . Where's the fifth one?"

"He's dead."

"How!?"

And Farha told him the story of Ezz al-Din the lamplighter, or the night imp, as they liked to refer to him among themselves. He had spent the evening with them as usual, and when it was time to go they left together. At the head of the street they stood to bid each other goodnight and take different roads, each to his own house. But on this particular night Farouk said, "It's summer, the weather's lovely—let's walk a bit."

"What's to go home for?" they answered easily.

They linked arms all together and crossed the railway track, heading toward Agriculture Street. Faris said, "Let's walk along the canal. The moon's light is filling the sky, and the air refreshes the soul."

They supported each other once more, until they reached the end of the road. There, they stood on the iron bridge looking down at the water flowing between its piers. Ezz al-Din said, "Who'll bet me I can't swim under the bridge?"

"We'll bet you," they answered in one breath. "How much?"

"A pound."

"Right."

They lifted him up onto the parapet, where he swayed for a while before spreading his arms wide, as the breeze filled his gallabiya. "One . . . two . . . three . . . here goes!"

He threw himself into the water, and they went to the other side of the bridge to wait for him to reappear. They stood there one hour, two hours, staring at the water, but he never surfaced. Then the dawn light broke, the bouza evaporated from their heads, and they threw dust on their faces and sobbed bitterly.

Poor Ezz al-Din was pulled out of the water three days later.

His corpse was washed up at a bridge twenty kilometers from the town, a perplexed expression on its face.

"God have mercy on his soul. So—where's your son Hamada?"

"Strange! You've never asked after him before."

"I want to speak to him about something."

"Are you planning to get married?"

"With that pile of flesh in the house?"

"God's blessings on their uncle!"

"I want him for a different marriage."

"Oh, who?"

"The lad Houda."

"The mute! And how come you're involved?"

"Maallim Osman asked me to take care of it."

"He'll turn up soon. Anyway, where were you this time?"

"God's lands are broad."

Abu Neama stood up among the wraiths, and headed for the shaykh. He grabbed his arm and pulled him toward him. "Come on, come and sit with us."

The shaykh raised the mug to his mouth and downed the contents in one. He wanted to lean back and put his legs up, but remembered he was sitting on a backless stool.

"Hayyy! Beauty of the Prophet!"

"You didn't asked about our absent friends."

"I just heard from Farha. My condolences on Ezz al-Din."

"And did you know what happened to Kaka?" said Abduh the barber.

"Oh, yes—there were six of you."

The shaykh stood up, gathered his quftan in his hands, put his prayer beads in his pocket, and sat down with them, leaning his back against the wall. The pale light of the bulb danced in front of his eyes, rising and falling, turning a complete circle in the ceiling, now maneuvering and changing color from green to red to

59

blue, now swinging from wall to wall, as though an insane hand had taken hold of the wire and was shaking it roughly about.

"What happened to Kaka?"

Abduh the barber, as an eyewitness, undertook to relate the tale as he had told it to the people of the town and in the police report, with careful precision and tedious detail. He chose to begin at the end. "God be merciful, he's in the hospital. But at least he's alive."

"Hospital!"

"He has gangrene in both legs."

"There is no power or strength but with God!"

Kaka the potter had withdrawn from life suddenly and stopped spending time with his friends. He no longer fired up his kiln, partly because there was now very little demand for the potter's art, and partly because the authorities waged war against it, as it apparently "polluted the environment"—even though it was sited on the edge of town. And on top of that, customers had switched to using plastic containers. They no longer needed pottery water jugs or pitchers, and could do without earthenware milk vessels, drainage pipes, or water jars—all these had become museum pieces of no use.

Kaka grew his beard and took up permanent residence in the market mosque. Then all at once it occurred to him—as though through heavenly inspiration—to demolish the kiln and destroy the remainder of his wares. He acquired a small plot of land, made bricks by hand, and brought in builders to construct a small prayer room, in which he worshiped alone once it was finished.

Then he stood among the people and announced, "Now you will witness the miracle."

He had collected a large pile of dried cotton stalks, which he doused with kerosene, and now he stood in the midst of them, shouting at the top of his voice, "Those present will tell those who are not that Kaka the prophet of God will not be harmed by the fire."

He pulled a match out of his pocket, struck it, and threw it into the firewood. He raised his arms to the sky, stroked his thick beard, dried the tears that were flowing copiously down his cheeks, and said, shaking, "Fire, be cool and wholesome on Kaka."

The fire caught the tail of his gallabiya, and spread to his drawers. He tried not to scream or cry for help, but the people grabbed him and plucked him out forcibly. They called an ambulance. He struggled and refused to be put on the stretcher, shouting in their faces, "Why have you deprived me of the miracle, you unbelievers?"

"There is no power or strength but with God!" The shaykh clapped one hand on the other. "The blasphemer wants to imitate the Father of the Prophets!"

"Don't say blasphemer."

"And don't say imitate."

"The Lord knows his secrets."

"Muhammad was the Seal of the Prophets—or have you forgotten that?"

"We haven't forgotten. It was a saintly act. And anyway, don't put yourself above us and start preaching—as if we needed that!"

"You're in the same boat as us. Aren't you a has-been mat-maker?"

"Plastic mats have finished you off."

Farha called to him from behind the counter. "Come over here, ya shaykh, and leave them to it."

He stood up to join her, brushing off the straw that clung to his quftan. Faris caught hold of him to stop him leaving, and to ask him sarcastically, "Haven't you heard of fitted carpet?"

"Luckily the mosques won't do without mats."

"They've put fitted carpet in, ya mawlana."

"So you didn't hear about Dahshan's donkey?"

61

The shaykh reminded them of the story. Dahshan starved his skinny donkey to punish it for tipping him and his load of clover onto the ground as he returned from the fields one evening. The donkey spent two days without food, sorrowfully watching the buffalo and the cow, to which Dahshan tossed a whole pile of the clover. He took them to the field, leaving the donkey tied up, so that it became depressed. Managing to break the hobble that bound its legs, it left the stable and went out onto the street, snuffling with its snout among the garbage, finding the stump of a cabbage, the stalk of a lettuce, or the peel of an orange, until it stood in front of the mosque. It saw the door was wide open, and since the sunset prayer was over and it was not yet time for the evening prayer, no one was there. The mosque was completely empty of worshipers. The donkey looked in and saw the new, green fitted carpet, extending like a well watered field of clover from the entrance to the prayer niche, so it stepped over the wooden threshold and nibbled at the carpet until it was sated. With nobody there to restrain it, it spent the time between the two prayers eating greedily until the muezzin arrived to make the call to evening prayer. He found it had finished off half the carpet, and instead of calling the faithful to prayer, he stood at the door and shouted, "Folks! Dahshan's donkey's eaten the fitted carpet!"

At the counter the shaykh found that Farha had refilled his mug. He raised it to his mouth and poured it down in one go. "Hayyy! Beauty of the Prophet!" He almost fell flat on his face, and Farha rushed to hold him up from behind.

"Pull yourself together. Here, sit down and try the snacks."

"I've got some important errands to run. I don't want to smell of fish and onions."

"Going to see a woman?"

"Those were the days! I'm past it now."

"It's the old hens that have the best fat."

"We just say those things to make ourselves feel better."

"Look—his lordship's arrived."

"Excuse me, I need to take him to one side."

Hamada held his hand out. "Good evening, ya shaykh."

"A very good evening to you."

The shaykh extricated himself from the wet handshake to take him in a long embrace, patting him on the back and feeling his soft shoulders, forearms, and waist. "My, you're fit and well." And he said to himself, "God's creation is infinite. The body of a woman, the touch of a woman—who put him in with the men?"

"I want a word with you."

"What is it?"

He towed him by the hand toward the entrance and examined his face under the lamp, whose pale light at first withdrew in defeat from the whiteness of the boy's complexion, and then shone, illuminated, and wrapped its pallor in brightness.

His eyebrows were plucked, his lips were lightly made up, and skin cream gave his cheeks a radiant softness. His partially revealed chest was hairless, and on the firm flesh hung a delicate gold chain. The brightly patterned shirt was tight at the waist and the sleeves were rolled up. Likewise, the broad-belted trousers were tight about his rounded buttocks, a prominent bulge at the front was restrained by a firm zipper, and at his feet the legs widened out to brush the floor in spite of the high heels of his shoes.

Since childhood, Hamada had taken pains over his appearance. Alone in the house, he never left the mirror. He washed his long, smooth hair and dried it with a hairdryer. He spent the whole day plucking out small facial hairs, and never gave his moustache the least chance to grow. He was patient in his attention to his body, and concerned for its cleanliness. He made a mixture of sugar and lemon juice to remove the hair on his legs, arms, and chest. A pair of tweezers was an essential tool, always in his pocket—when he was preoccupied or worried about something he would take them between his thumb and finger and tensely draw out little hairs.

His mother was not interested in his private world. She had asked God for a child, and he had answered her. It did not matter if it was a boy or a girl. She had lived with her late husband for ten years, and had buried many of her premature babies in paupers' graves—and that was besides her numerous miscarriages, which she buried under the floor in the house. Her husband died when Hamada was a bloody cluster multiplying in her womb.

When he emerged into the world, his grandmother, who had been running the bouza shop for many years, seized him, saying, "We'll sell him to a devout holy man, to look after him in his own way."

Farha acquiesced to every charm she heard from the neighborhood women.

"You must eat some of his feces."

"All right." And she swallowed the morsel without hesitation.

"Drink the milk of a donkey."

"All right." They milked the neighbors' jenny, and she tossed it down with no sign of aversion.

"Find a bitch that's just given birth, and drink its milk."

It was quite difficult to milk a bitch, but the grandmother held the snout while Farha bent down to the full dugs and pulled on one after the other to dribble some of the milk into her mouth.

The boy lived, and thrived between his mother and his grandmother. With an earring in his ear, and wearing girls' clothes, he was not harmed by the evil eye.

When her mother passed on, Farha was obliged to work in the bouza shop. She would leave her only child at home, and he became as proficient at housework as any clever girl. He would sweep, cook, change the beds, and wash. This was all a mercy to his mother, who spent her nights running the shop and her days asleep or preparing the bouza for the evening.

Before his grandmother died, Hamada became caught up in the world of the dancing girls who landed in town at mulid time. They would spend some of their evenings at the bouza shop. His body responded to the rhythm of the drum and the tambourine, his pleasant voice became sweeter as he sang along with their songs, and he imitated their movements and gestures.

After a while, the mulid was no longer enough for him, and he journeyed with them on their travels to Mansoura, Sinbillawayn, Mit Ghamr, Tanta, and distant Banha. A week would go by without his mother seeing him, and then his absences grew longer and he would stay away a month or more. His mother told him, "Make yourself a band here and work with me."

"In this miserable town? I need to broaden my range."

When she opened his bags she was astonished to discover skimpy women's clothing in screaming colors. "What's the boy doing with women's underwear? And off-the-shoulder, open-back, split-leg dresses?"

Should she believe what the wagging tongues repeated? Why not? The boy was like a woman in all particulars—both in his adornment of his body and in his shunning of male company. He could not bear to sit with the men here. What confirmed the rumors for her was finding decorated boxes of beauty tools. He was quite brazen about it, and did not care what anybody thought or said. His mother gave in and accepted the situation— she was just happy to have him around, her only companion in the world.

"Look, young man, we need you for a job on Thursday."

"But I have a booking on Thursday."

"Have they paid you yet?"

"I took a deposit."

"Give them the deposit back—we'll give you plenty more than that."

"A wedding?"

"To tell you the truth, no."

"I only do weddings."

"A little acting job."

"Acting? I've never acted before."

"This time we want you to act."

The shaykh explained everything, at great length. Whenever Hamada raised an objection, the shaykh let him finish, then went on to hammer his point home. In the end he convinced him, and the boy finally asked who the groom was.

"Houda the mute."

"Those mutes are vicious—he might do something to me."

"Everyone will be around you. Everything is planned."

"Okay. How much are you paying?"

"Whatever you say. Maallim Osman is taking care of everything from A to Z."

"I need two hundred in advance, for the hairdresser, the clothes, and so on."

"You'll have it in the morning. Good night."

The wraiths raised their shaky hands without producing any intelligible sound, then turned back to each other to continue their intimate conversation that had no link to the world of today.

Farha came out from behind the counter, wiping her hands on the sides of her gallabiya. "It's early yet."

"No, it's about time." He held out what he owed her.

"Oh, no, ya shaykh, it's paid for."

"This one's on me, Ma."

"It looks like you agreed on a peach of a wedding celebration."

"Something like that."

"May you live long, my friend, and fill the world with celebrations."

The shaykh thanked Hamada for agreeing to take part, as well as for paying his tab, and raised his hand in farewell. Collecting his quftan around his big belly, and extracting the long string of prayer-beads, which he set going between his fingers, he went out of the door and into the dark street.

6

*A*t the bridge, he considered sending one of the young motor-bike riders to buy his hashish from one of the small villages, but thought better of it because they were so rapacious in the share they took of the merchandise, biting off an eighth or a quarter of it before rewrapping it carefully in its cellophane paper.

They lined up here night and day, near the main gate of the railway station, waiting for the trains and cars, transporting the people of the neighboring villages behind them on their bikes. They wore leather jackets, hard helmets on their heads, and cheap dark glasses on their faces.

As he walked past them, one of them approached him. "A very good evening to you, ya shaykh. Can I do anything for you?"

"No thanks, son."

"The villages have some first-rate stuff this week. I just brought Hagg Disouqi the salted fish merchant a really great piece." He held his thumb up in front of the shaykh's face.

"No thanks, brother. I'm all right for now."

He crossed the rails embedded in the black basalt chips and headed downhill in the opposite direction, walking in darkness punctuated every now and then by the light of a lost lamp. "God damn it, all the council's lampposts are burned out."

He went on stumbling in potholes or stepping in puddles of water and finally emerged into the light of Zizi's café. He stood to one side until he could beckon to Zizi's wife, standing at the counter.

"God! The same old faces." He felt the tedium gripping at his throat. The town was stuck in a rut. This was the only place on earth where nothing changed. Every café had its regulars—if you wanted a particular person, you didn't tire yourself out looking for him, you just sent a boy to So-and-so's café: he would be sitting there and would come to you right away.

Zizi's wife came out drying her hands on the sides of her gallabiya. "Is that your face or the face of the moon? No wonder it's so light! Come on in!"

"I can't, I'm sorry, I have to get on. So where's Ismail?"

"Of course, you've been away. May the Lord release him."

"Again!"

"As long as that crap is around, do you think he'll give it up?"

"It's a good living, woman."

"And what about the pile of flesh he's left me with—what am I supposed to do with them? Ammour, boy!"

A small, naked-bottomed child came crawling on hands and knees out of the warmth of the café and climbed up the step to the street, his face filthy and his gallabiya torn at both sides. The shaykh thrust his hand into the pocket of his quftan and held it out to the child. "Here, little fellow."

The boy snarled and cleaved to his mother's gallabiya, hiding his face and kicking his leg out at the shaykh.

"Take it from the shaykh, boy! His money's a blessing."

The boy snatched the ten-piaster coin quickly and hid again in his mother's skirts.

"Is that the one?"

"Yes, that's him—remember?"

He had been sitting with Ammour, Maallim Osman's apprentice, as she squatted in front of them holding the goza and lifting off the tobacco bowl to throw the cinders in the old vegetable ghee can, her belly stretched far out in front of her. She was not uncomfortable or in pain, and carried on working hard, between seeing to things at the counter and serving the customers. Her husband was in prison then too.

When the shaykh raised the reed to his mouth, the coals crackled and the fire burned hotter on the tobacco. He leaned back, inebriated by the dope. "Beauty of the Beloved Prophet!"

Then as he leaned forward again he saw the piece of flesh fall between her legs. Ammour, on the point of leaving behind his last scrap of focused attention and entering the fog of mindless intoxication, where reality and fantasy meet, said, "Pick the boy up off the ground."

Rocking on his seat, the shaykh said, echoing the popular song, "Give the boy to his father."

Zizi's wife realized what had happened, lifted her gallabiya so that the blood would not soil it, picked up the newborn in her arms, and disappeared behind the counter. Ammour woke her older daughters, asleep in a corner of the café, to take over from their mother.

"And why didn't you call him after me? I was there too."

"We're poor folk, and we give poor folk's names."

"He's not his son, is he, girl?"

"Don't talk rot! Nobody steps on my toes. I'm more of a man than him—do you think he can sleep with a man?"

"Ismail often spends a long time in jail."

"Even if he spent his whole life there! Get on with you, ya mawlana. You're treading on thin ice, and I haven't got time for you. If you want to sit down, you're welcome. If you don't, on your bike. People are trying to make a living here."

"Look after yourself."

"Buy from Nisnas. He's at his house near the church."

"I was on my way there."

He left the meager light for the dark, walking slowly, staying close to the walls of the houses so that he could lean on them when he needed to. The light of Samara's café erupted after a short while. Its brightness dazzled him and turned the men sitting in two rows into ghosts—he saw their shapes but could not make out their features, though he heard their cries from both sides.

"Come and join us!"

"Come and join us, ya mawlana. Come and have a quick smoke!"

He raised both his arms to greet the two sides, and his gallabiya and quftan dropped together to the ground, so he was obliged to hitch them up with one hand and pay respects with the other. Then he had to withdraw even that hand to hold his nose, as he could not bear the smell of the garlic Samara's son was frying up with pieces of blackened liver in the upturned lid of a cooking pot on a tin stand shielding a stove that gave out more soot than flame.

He steered his stout body off to the left and came to the closed door of the church. Lamplight shone from inside and then was lost behind the tall poplars and eucalyptuses, while a light also glowed in the belfry, which towered over the ramshackle old houses that surrounded the church. The whole building was squeezed in among these houses, which closed in on it and left no space between them but the narrow streets that were wide enough for just one person.

He took the street to the right and was once more enveloped in darkness. He ran his left hand along the stone wall of the church, wary of falling into the entrances to the doors of the houses, which were like great holes that drew one in by force. After he had passed three doors he went up to a window in whose apertures were trapped both light and smoke. He knocked with the knuckle of his index finger, but no one answered, so he cleared his throat and shouted loudly, "Ya Nisnas!"

There was no reply. He put his mouth to one of the openings of the window and called in a low voice, "It's me, Shaykh Saadoun."

One leaf of the window was opened cautiously, and the head of Nisnas poked out. He stared lengthily at the shaykh's face, examined his whole body from turban to shoe, and said quietly and without enthusiasm, "Hello, ya shaykh."

"Asleep?"

"Resting a bit."

"Here." And he gave him the usual amount of money.

"What do you want?"

"I want to gaze at your beauty."

"That doesn't cover it. Seems you haven't smoked anything in a long time."

"Only every bloody day."

"Give me the same again."

"It's for Maallim Osman."

"He knows the price. Happy new year—the stuff'll be extinct soon."

"The growers won't stop growing it, the sellers won't stop selling it, and the smokers certainly won't stop smoking it."

"It'll make way for another product that's cheaper."

"Stop philosophizing, hand over the smokes, and let me be on my way."

"Give me another tenner."

"All that fuss for ten piasters, you scumbag?"

"A tenner means ten pounds."

"Great God! Take it and be damned."

"What skin is it off your nose? He's paying for it."

"What am I, a sponger?"

"You tell me. Mind how you go, now."

"It'd better not be doctored."

"As God is your witness, have you ever had a doctored smoke from me?"

"Well, no. But where's the bit of opium? So I can say a prayer for you."

Nisnas held out a twist the size of a dried chickpea to the shaykh, who quickly pressed it under his tongue and set off in the direction of Abu Ashour's house.

The two narrow streets that contain the church end in a slightly wider street that leads to a square, in the middle of which stands the tomb of Abu Zeina. As Shaykh Saadoun approached it he raised his right hand, gripping the string of prayer beads, to lean with it on the window frame, and bent his head humbly to contemplate the shrine dressed in green silk, drenched in a light from a hidden source that eliminated all shadows. There was the great head turbaned in a white shawl with decorated fringes that dangled on both sides, glowing and shining in the bright circle of light that showed up the precise black lettering on the sides of the shrine.

The shaykh recited the opening chapter of the Quran to himself, then wiped his face with his hand and awoke from the withdrawal of the soul that always affected him when he stood at the tomb of one of the devout friends of God. He stepped back, and pinched his nostrils. "God damn this town." He looked around for someone to scold, a neighbor of the tomb, but all the doors and windows were shut, and the square was completely quiet. How can they let their children shit under the walls of a holy site like this? How do they even let their women throw out their dirty water and vegetable scraps? They're lucky to live under the holy man's protection, and he's so forgiving that he hasn't taken anyone to task for what they do—and he's well able to do so. Look how neglected the tomb is, and the owner of the tomb. By rights it should have been incorporated in a fine mosque, but

73

these miserable people have left it no more than a large dome on four walls, half buried in the ground, the windowledge level with the street. We should have to look up to it, not bend over to look down on it.

He gathered the edges of his quftan in his fist and left. The moment of revelation that had seized his heart had been extinguished, and he wiped the tears from his eyes on the crumpled rag of a handkerchief that he kept in his pocket.

Then suddenly he heard a shout echo around the square. "Ya Saadoun!" He looked all around him, but saw no one. He fixed his eyes on the intense white light that shone on the green of the shrine, as it seemed to him that the call had come from behind the window.

"Ya Saadoun!"

He blinked, but the bright light prevented him from seeing anything. He stood for a long time, trying to make out who was calling, but it did not come again. He turned to his right into a side street.

Here the streets broadened out and became regular, because this was the end of the old town and the beginning of the new town that had been built on agricultural land after the farmers had moved out. The owner had sold it off piecemeal, each plot big enough for a house. Abu Ashour's was the last of the houses that gave their back to the old town and faced onto the new. Not so long ago it stood on the fringe and its door and windows opened onto the fields, receiving the delicate breezes of the night, and allowing the light of the moon to linger until the first hours of the day.

Behind the window half open at the top, the shaykh heard the voices of the men mingling with the voice of the reciter on the owner's radio, which he always kept to hand and never changed the station from the Glorious Quran. He would leave it on in the background until something caught his attention, then he would repeat the last few verses and ask the men sitting around to explain them, which they were always unable to do. Abu Ashour would then go on to offer his own explanation, as he stepped back, leaned against the wall, inhaled deeply, stroked his long beard, shook his emaciated turbaned head, closed his eyelids over his kohled eyes, and began rapturously, "Listen, my friends. . . ," as he drew on his elastic knowledge.

Shaykh Saadoun knocked on the closed leaf of the window.

"Yes!"

He recognized the voice of Qunsul, who stood to open the door for him cautiously. The shaykh greeted the men and removed his shoes before stepping on the rush mat spread on the floor of the room. He spotted Maallim Osman sitting under the window, so he squeezed his great body in beside him. The maallim asked him, "How did you get on?"

"Let me get my breath first."

"Have you seen a ghost or something?"

"Well, aren't you going to say 'Welcome back'?" He was addressing Abu Ashour, who was busy cleaning and filling the tobacco bowls in the wooden racks lined up in front of him. His face was masked behind the steam of the big kettle that was pressed into the hot sand box over a primus stove that never ceased hissing.

"When you learn to give the Islamic greeting first."

The shaykh called on the men to back him up. "Did I say 'Salamu alaykum' or not?"

Everybody affirmed that he had indeed given the greeting before he had taken off his shoes.

"Tell that to this crook."

"A crook, am I? Looks like you're ready to start something."

"Let me get my puff."

75

"Take your puffs first." And Qunsul, who was squatting in front of Maallim Osman, held the reed out to the shaykh, after the maallim had waved it away. The shaykh grabbed it and began pulling deeply on it, as the small brands jumped around on the tobacco bowl and fell off onto the mat, to be chased down by Qunsul with the tongs before they did too much damage. The old mat was already full of black burn marks, as were the cotton long johns that strangled Qunsul's skinny shanks. He was leaning with his forearm on one leg, while the other was folded under him to make room for the wooden rack and the sieve blazing with live coals.

"A fine evening to you, ya mawlana."

He tipped the spent tobacco bowl into the tin can and picked up a fresh full one to secure it on the neck of the goza. Then he shook the sieve in front of him professionally to concentrate the fire, blew off the light ash, and tipped it onto the bowl, arranging the glowing brands with his dry fingers. He offered the reed to Maallim Osman, but once again he pushed it in the shaykh's direction.

"Get the shaykh stoned first, so we can all have a good time."

Abu Ashour, having picked up a verse from the chanting on the radio, pounced on him. "Explain that one, ya shaykh: *It said: You ants, you better get home, or else Solomon will squash you with his feet.*"

"You ignoramus, recite the verse properly: *An ant exclaimed: O ants! Enter your dwellings lest Solomon and his armies crush you, unperceiving.*"

"I understand it, anyway: There's this little ant out walking with its mates, minding its own business, and all of a sudden it sees the Prophet Solomon coming along with his army. So it says to them, 'Watch out, get out of his way, or he'll squash you with his feet.' And God blessed the Prophet Solomon with the power to speak with the birds and the animals, and even the ants."

"Oh, very good. Really, well done."

76

The men bellowed and staggered backward, clapping their hands. Abu Ashour stiffened, sniffed back his snot, and wiped his moustacheless upper lip. His tattooed hand shook as he poured the tea into the mug. He leaned across the sand box to pass the tray to the customer, who said merrily, "May God give you more of his knowledge!"

The shaykh puffed the smoke from his nostrils, keeping some of it back to hold it in his lungs. He coughed, leaned back to take out the handkerchief rolled up in his pocket, spat in it, and addressed the men. "Before anything else, he should recite the words of the Lord correctly."

Abu Ashour was not going to let this pass. "So where did this happen?"

"Where did what happen?"

"When Joseph's brothers threw him in the well, and a driver came along who needed water for his engine, which had over-heated. He threw a bucket down the well, and Joseph was sitting down there in the water, so when he saw the bucket he grabbed hold of the rope. The driver pulled from the top of the well and found the bucket had gotten very heavy. He kept on pulling till he found Joseph—just a small kid—coming up out of the water. Well, he fainted right away."

"Listen to this imbecile. What are you on about, a driver? Did they have cars in those days?"

"The shaykh's blaspheming against the word of God, guys! Well, explain the noble verse: *And there came traffic, and they sent their waterdrawer. He let down his pail. He said: Good luck! Here is a youth. And they hid him as a treasure, and God was aware of what they did.*"

"What does 'traffic' mean, folks?"

"Cars, of course."

"Tell our blaspheming brother here. I served in that region in the Palestine War, and the same thing that happened to Joseph's driver happened to me. I was an ace driver, so they picked me to drive the general's car. One day, the car overheated, and I came to a well, the spitting image of Joseph's well, because the land there isn't watered by canals and channels like ours is, no, it's all watered from wells from under the ground. Anyway, I threw the bucket down the well and pulled it as hard as I could—and that's when I thought of our lord Joseph."

"'Traffic'—you numbskull—means people walking on foot."

"By the Prophet, who's convinced by such talk? Am I supposed to forget the word of God and go along with the shaykh?"

"It's up to you—go along with whoever you please."

Maallim Osman smiled at the shaykh and nudged him, goading him to continue the conversation. He was never happier than when watching the skirmishing of these two men, and whenever the flame died out he would broach a new topic to set them at odds. Each would proclaim he was right, and each wanted to show off his prowess in front of these men whose features were obscured behind thick clouds of smoke.

"Well, try this, ya mawlana."

"What?"

"On the Day of Resurrection, everyone will point at one man and say, 'That's our father Adam.' They'll all know him by one distinguishing feature. What is it?"

"He'll be the only one without a navel, because he wasn't born of a woman, like the rest of creation."

The men acclaimed this with cries of "God is great!"

Abu Ashour scowled, threw the tobacco bowl he was cleaning in their direction, and snapped, "Hold on a minute, you simpletons! You want to applaud a mistake?"

"What mistake, ya Abu Ashour? It's as obvious as the sun."

Qunsul stood up from changing the water in the goza, and turned to them. "Be patient—my father has another explanation."

"Our father Adam had a navel."

"How's that, ya Abu Ashour?"

"When the Lord God Almighty had made him out of mud, but before he blew the breath of life into him, he left him in the sun for a while, for the mud to dry. Along came accursed Satan, strolling through Paradise—he hadn't rebelled yet, you see—and he saw Adam stretched out in front of him. He didn't know who he was, so he poked his finger in his belly, asking himself, 'What's this?' And that was the start of the navel."

"You mean our navel is Satan's finger?"

"Exactly."

The shaykh paused. He had been busy extracting the piece of hashish from its cellophane wrapper, and biting it in his teeth, to put it under the maallim's nose. "The man's raving."

"Okay, putting aside the business of the navel," Maallim Osman asked Abu Ashour, "how will the people know?"

"I'm glad you asked me that. By the empty bit in his chest."

"What bit, reverend shaykh?" asked Shaykh Saadoun sarcastically.

"Where the rib was that the Lord made our mother Eve from."

"Oh, go break a rib of your own. Send a refill over here, and stop talking nonsense."

"See, folks, he said nonsense."

"Does that mean you're giving in, ya shaykh?"

"You bunch of idiots, he's making fools of you. He's doing this to keep your heads clear so that you blithely smoke all night while he fills his pocket. It's a brilliant ruse, but it doesn't wash with me."

"It still means you're giving in."

"Fine, I'm giving in, but I live to fight another day. Qunsul, set up the goza, and tell your father to keep quiet. I want to have a serious talk with this fellow," he said, indicating Maallim Osman.

The men settled down and began minor conversations in subdued voices. Abu Ashour busied himself with his work, scooping cold water out of the metal barrel and pouring it into the kettle pressed in the hot sand. When Qunsul threw him a rack of empties, he took out each bowl, cleaned it of the burned honey-tobacco, kept the stone to put it back in the throat of the bowl, stuffed the bowl again with sticky tobacco from the large plastic container, and stacked up the racks in a rising edifice. Qunsul took one after the other, as he moved among the groups of men spread around the shabby mat. The voice of the Quran reciter on the radio stood out, and every now and then Abu Ashour would break the silence with a shout of "Proclaim the unity of God!" Qunsul watched him carefully, worried that the ecstasy would suddenly take hold of him, and he would be stretched out unconscious behind the sand box. He would then go over to him to splash his face with cold water and put a peeled onion under his nose, at which he would thrash about and flail his arms. Qunsul would grasp his arms while sitting on his legs, so that he didn't knock over the boiling pot whose steam mixed with the smoke of the dope. Abu Ashour would wake from his faint in surprise. He would retie his loosened turban, wipe the tears that ran with kohl down his cheeks with his sleeve, and rub his nose with the back of his hand. When he was settled on his cushion he would look around at the sitting men, who were accustomed to his sudden collapses. Not one of them would move, and he would yell at them accusingly, "Well, bless the Beloved Prophet!"

"God bless him."

And once again he would become engrossed in his work, treating his ears to the sound of the chanting on the radio.

Maallim Osman whispered in the shaykh's ear, "How did you get on?"

"Just fine."

Qunsul had moved on to another group. The maallim, who had been warming the brown lump in his hands, cut some small pieces off it and lined them up on a sheet of clean white paper. The shaykh went on. "I met the boy and fixed it with him. Everything's fine."

"He agreed?"

"How could he refuse?

"You have his mother in the palm of your hand."

"By God, she doesn't know what I want him for. When she asked me, I told her we wanted him to sing at a wedding."

"Well done."

"The important thing now is to get the room ready for him to take his bride to, and to arrange for the car for the procession. And you have to talk to the hairdresser, so that he treats the boy like any ordinary bride. And later we have to see about the things to be put in the basket for the bridal supper."

"That's all taken care of."

"You're a man who gets things done, ya maallim!"

"It must all be kept a complete secret."

"Don't forget the boy's deaf and dumb."

"Deaf and dumb? You're the one who's deaf and dumb! By God, I'll teach him!"

Wedding Day

1

What a spin your head is in, ya Houda! Two women in one! How did you leave behind your miserable bed to get there? How were you transported after the dawn call to prayer?

You were waiting for your brother to wake up. When he rose at his usual time, you wanted to get up too, even though he signed to you: Stay home—that's what the maallim said—it's your wedding day. Get yourself ready until I come back this afternoon.

You were not aware of anything after that. You don't know how he washed his face, picked up his gear, and closed the door behind him, as he did every day. You surrendered to sweet sleep. At this time of the day you were usually outside, so it was quite novel for you to spend the time in bed. Sleep drew you down into its deep well, and passed you from dream to dream until you saw yourself there, climbing the shaded staircase. You found her waiting for you in her see-through silk dress and her scent that made your head spin, with her short hair falling over her brow in an arousing style. She opened her arms to you and led you into a large room you had seen from the outside but had never set foot in.

There was nothing of the maallim here.

Your hand gave in to her hand, soft and gentle.

In the bedroom, she let her clothes fall to the floor, one piece after another, and she signaled to you: Come up here. And . . . and you found yourself totally and completely naked under the mosquito net. She became the universe itself, and when you were writhing on top of her you saw Fakiha's face on the same body. The two faces interchanged, appeared, and disappeared, and you were perplexed: which one should you fix in place?

The two-faced body enervated you, and through your confusion you could not settle on anything. You fell on your face, worn out, and woke up gasping for breath on the pillow that was spotted with blood from the fleas. You shifted the position of your exhausted but excited body. You lay on your back to observe the sunlight that invaded the gaps in the wood of the high window of your room overlooking the street. You had never seen the morning sun in this room before.

So, come on and greet your new day. Thank God you didn't waste your seed in that strenuous dream. You stood up and stretched in unaccustomed luxury, and splashed water from the zinc tap over your face, drying it with the remains of a towel thrown on Zaki's bed. You pushed open both halves of the window, and the light was unleashed, its strong rays gushing in, dancing specks of dust suspended in it. The unsightliness of the room and the wretchedness of its mean contents became plain. You shoved the last of the cheese between the two pieces of bread that Zaki had left for your breakfast, and chewed on that as you pushed the padlock into the rusty clasp.

The Azhar student's room was closed up—he must have left for his institute, then. You saw blind Aida with her sister Nawal mounting the stairs, carrying a bundle of pastry they had brought back from the cemetery this morning. Thus the day unfolded, in the opposite direction to normal.

What would Fakiha be doing at this time of day? Had she gone to the market to buy vegetables? Or would you see her squatting in her room, spending the long day waiting for Fikri to return from work? Why don't you have a peek through her window?

You remembered the bizarre dream, and you were aroused once more.

—Nearly there.

Tonight you will put an end to the frenzy of desire. Tonight you will come to know the body of a mystery woman.

—What does it matter? I trust the maallim's taste. He has experience with women, no one can deny that. Just look at his new wife—is there any woman more beautiful in the whole town? Sure, he won't pick me someone with quite her looks, but at least he'll pick someone reasonable.

Whether you meant to or not, you craned your neck to look into Fakiha's room, and you saw her taking off her black over-gallabiya and throwing her headscarf on the sofa.

—She's just come back from the market.

Shaking her head to free one of her earrings from a lock of hair, she caught sight of you. You wanted to retreat in embarrassment, even though you saw her—quite unusually—smiling at you. You allowed your eyes to gaze at her for a long time, and the smile didn't leave her face. In fact, she stared back at you, and your eyes remained hooked to hers until they lost their focus, and your vision became indistinct and foggy.

She raised her arm toward you. "Well, are you going to stand like that all day?" She signed to you, making her left fist into a mug and the index finger of her right hand a spoon to stir it: "Cup of tea?"

The blood surged in your veins, but you were surprised to find your hand coming up to the side of your head to say, "No, thank you."

She turned her back to the door and said, pouting, "If it's No, thank you, it's No, thank you. Up to you."

You stood there confounded. Should you go out to the street, or go back to her, and let her know you really would like some tea?

Why didn't you think before answering? This was the first clear invitation she had given you. What an ass you are—you missed your chance.

Your feet dragged, your step faltered. You stood at the big door onto the street, observing its life at a time of day you had never known before. The shade of the mulberry trees was enticing to sit under. A little later, maybe, the women would meet there, helping each other to clean the vegetables or to pick the small stones out of the rice, as they would begin cooking after the midday prayer. You felt the hand touch your shoulder and turned around to see that the smile had not left her face—she wanted to get past you to go out with her bag of vegetables, while you wanted to constrict the sturdy body in the half-open leaf of the door. You indicated that she should pass in front of you, but she declined and signaled that you should step down out of the way because there wasn't room for her to squeeze through.

You signed to her that you had changed your mind and would like to have that cup of tea, but she replied coquettishly, "Another time."

You asked her when that would be. "When the cows come home," she signed, as she crossed the street.

She walked away from you to sit in the shade, and you left the doorway, sighing. You said to yourself, "Why should I care about this woman? My bride might be more beautiful than her, anyway, or perhaps at least as beautiful. If she is, I'll kiss the maallim's hand, and let him use my face as a doormat forever." And you headed off for Market Street.

You made a complete circuit of the wall of the big house, enjoying the shade of its luxuriant green trees that leaned over the road, before leaving it near its southern gate to enter a narrow side street that opened onto the teeming Market Street, where you walked among the open shops.

The saddler had hung his tools outside, but did not leave his place in the dark of the shop, the ninety-nine beads of the prayer string in his hands, the wooden stand in front of him supporting the open, gold-bound copy of the Quran before which he rocked forward and backward, chanting verses in a low voice. He would rise only to give the call to prayer from the minaret of the market mosque—but only the midday, afternoon, and sunset prayers, after which he would retire to his house, leaving the evening and dawn prayers to Blind Amin.

He lifted his head slightly, waved his white hand with the prayer beads, and gave you a kind, friendly smile. You returned it and called out to him in a loud voice, "Ab . . . ab." And you pointed to the sky, so he raised his hands in front of his face and prayed for you.

You passed by the cobbler, the seed merchant, and the mat-maker, and stopped to watch Farouk the blacksmith lifting the sledgehammer high with his strong arm, to let it fall on the incandescent iron, striking it powerfully to make a mattock head to turn the earth, or a sickle to harvest the crops, or a chisel to cut the millstones.

When he saw you he stopped work, buried the tip of the iron in the glowing coals in front of the mouth of the bellows, and signaled to his apprentice to pull on the rope, tied through a pulley in the ceiling, that lifted the great lung of the bellows and forced the compacted air over the fire. The boy hung from the ring on the rope, and gravity brought him down again. Meanwhile, Farouk stood making signs of congratulation, and signaling that he would finish work before sunset, go home to clean the soot from his face and hands, and put on his best gallabiya to lead the well-wishers at the wedding—and he indicated with his arms the shops to both sides. You raised your hand to your head to thank him.

As you left his shop your eyes fell on Faris, standing in his large, baggy undertrousers and his many-buttoned waistcoat fastened over his chest. He was leaning with his whole body on a long saw sunk halfway through a tender tree trunk, his bare feet planted on the bark of the trunk, which was stretched between two wooden trestles at either end. He wiped the sweat from his forehead and smiled happily at you. Removing his turban, he said he was going to spend all night with the dancing girls—he kissed his bunched fingers—and he had heard that the maallim had engaged the two most beautiful dancers in the land. Then he signed that he would invite you to a mug of bouza, to lend courage to your heart so that you would go in to your bride without trepidation. You signed back that you didn't need the bouza, that you had plenty of courage, praise be to God, and that you would be honored by his and everybody else's attendance at the wedding.

Faris, spitting in his palms, went back to his recalcitrant saw to cut into the heart of the living log.

You passed the insecticides store, and Tuhami's café, and Mikkawi's soft drinks factory, and stopped in front of Abu Neama's tailoring shop. You found him there behind the low bench, cutting a piece of material spread out before him. His apprentices were around him, the oldest one leaning over the black head of a Singer sewing machine, another one gripping the braid between his toes and sewing it with a fine needle around the neck of a woolen gallabiya, and a third watching them all and waiting for their orders to pass the scissors to this one or the tape measure to that one, or to be sent out on an errand to buy buttons or braid or to go to the buttonhole-maker's shop for him to cut the holes.

You greeted them with a movement of your hand and stuttered some inarticulate sounds. "Ar . . . ar."

Abu Neama looked up at you, lifting his broad head, and the blood rushed to his fleshy cheeks as he was filled with delight. "Welcome to the groom!"

He gestured for you to sit on the empty chair, but you replied that you were busy and had to run a hundred errands—but had he finished the wedding gallabiya? Abu Neama signaled to one of his lads to fetch the white gallabiya folded up in the cupboard, and the boy brought it very carefully draped across his outstretched arms. He asked you, "Do you want to try it on for size?"

You tossed your hand in the air testily, and signed that you had already tried the size more than once. You kissed your hand and made an imaginary handshake in the air, to say, "God bless your clever fingers!"

He signaled to you that instead of going home, he would stay on working until it was time for the wedding, then he would take his lads along there, as he and his friends from the bouza shop had all agreed on having a truly fine night out. You pushed your head down into the raised collar of your gallabiya and signed "Thank you" as you left. Then you remembered something, and went back to ask him how much it would be. He clapped one hand on the other and told you, "The maallim's a good man—it's all paid for." He pointed to his moustache and spread his soft hand on his belly. You walked out backward, raising your face to the ceiling of the shop—"Ab . . . ab"—entreating God to add to the maallim's blessings.

You passed the potter's shop, and Shukuku's café, and the grocer's. The smell of the incense rising with the smoke coming from al-Adal's salon met your nostrils. You saw him behind the glass of the door, with his huge face supporting his unruly gray hair, his dense moustache of dark hairs spreading over his cheeks, yellowed in a thin streak under his nose. He stood there, his terrific frame in a gallabiya under which he wore nothing, summer or winter. His belly stuck out in front of him, keeping him at a distance from the customer whose head was bent forward in surrender to the electric trimmer shaving the hair on the back of his neck.

You opened one leaf of the door, and the smell became stronger, as you noticed the incense stick wedged in a crack in the wooden table that had the hairdressing equipment on it. Al-Adal turned to you. "Here's the sorry excuse for a groom!"

You didn't understand the meaning of the words, but anyway you submitted to his gesture that said, "Sit down till I finish what I'm doing."

The customer raised his head for a while to breathe, until al-Adal returned it to its original position by covering the shaven dome with his broad hand and pushing it down to rest on the man's chest, moving closer to blow away the hairs that had fallen on the back of his scalp. He picked up the trimmer, rolled up his broad sleeves again, and made a vulgar sign to you, which you understood to mean, "Finally you're going to be a man. You're going to have fun tonight with a bride the envy of every lad in town."

You signed to him to get on with his work so that he could see to you and give you a proper groom's grooming, which would certainly take a long time, as you wanted your hair cut, your cheeks plucked, your eyebrows trimmed, your chin shaved, your fingernails clipped, and all such as that. Al-Adal put out his hand to lift up your gallabiya, and said, with the insolence people expected of him, "And we'll shave your pubes into the bargain."

The customer laughed at the crude fun, but you screamed at him—"Arb . . .. arb!"—put your new gallabiya down on the chair, and closed your hands about his throat to pull his head from his body. He pretended to scream and held his hands up. "I'm dying! Houda's murdering me!"

Your hands fell to your sides from the effort, but still he would not leave you alone. He grasped your head and dragged it in front of the mirror. "What shall I do with you? Shall I turn it round the other way? So you sleep with your bride ass-first?"

Your neck hurt hard, so you punched him in the belly, but your hands bounced off as if they had hit a reinforced wall. You blew on them, grumbling, and al-Adal said spitefully, "You spineless wonder! I know you're going to let us down tonight."

He pulled the customer out of the chair and lifted you up into it. "There you go. We'll do what we can, and the rest's up to God."

Now you saw your gaunt, dark face in the wide, clear mirror. A face drawn and strained, the eyes sunken in the skull, the cheekbones sticking out, the cheeks themselves two hollow cavities.

Al-Adal wrapped the towel around your skinny neck, and you signed to him to shave your face and remove the fuzz around your eyes and eyebrows and on your ears. He pointed to his eyes in a gesture of acquiescence. "Whatever you say." And he signed, "If you want me to come with you to the house to bath you and scrub you down, I'm more than willing."

You thumped him with your elbow in his taut belly.

When he was finished, you held out the money you owed him, but he declined it. When you insisted, he refused, and it ended with him signing to you, "I'll sort it out with the maallim. There's still the henna and the public procession, and a long night to come."

Should you go back to your room? The day still stretched ahead, and you were trying to resist the temptation to see the new place that you would move into tonight. Were you to lock yourself up in your room and wait, though?

You felt like heading to Mitwalli's café for a proper start to the morning. But would you be sure to find a customer? Perhaps a quick look there would decide it. Then you wanted to drop in at the butcher's shop to make sure of the preparations for the wedding. But you were afraid the maallim would close the subject at once, and you would be no better off. You might be able to signal to Zaki from a distance, but that bastard would scowl in your face and shout, "You never stop doubting. You've given me a headache with your pestering."

But you wouldn't relax until you knew for certain that things were going as you wanted them to.

At Mitwalli's, everybody jumped up to see you, and gathered around, clapping and dancing about in circles. These were the service taxi drivers and their lads who called out for customers, along with the motorbike riders in their leather clothes, crash helmets, and large sunglasses. They dragged Aziza into the center of the ring, and one of them took the scarf from his neck and tied it around her hips, as somebody else grabbed a metal serving tray and began drumming on it with his strong fingers. Adenoidal Aziza responded to the rhythm and shook her body, lifting her hands up to her head, and they shoved you forward to dance with her. You complied shyly. Mitwalli stood at the counter happily watching the dance.

You noticed Nisnas in a corner of the café, laughing heartily until a coughing fit overtook him. His body resounded with it, as his face turned red, and every now and then he bent over to hawk onto the sawdust floor, treading the phlegm in with his slipper.

When Aziza came to a stop, she withdrew from the circle, and you followed her, panting from the effort. The men broke up and sat down on the chairs, shouting boisterously. You didn't understand the meaning of the winks in your direction or the clapping of palm against palm, so you ignored them and went over to Nisnas and squatted next to him. He knew what you wanted and patted you kindly on the back, then signaled to Mitwalli to bring you some tea. You added to this by placing your thumb on the middle of your index finger, and Mitwalli understood that you wanted half a glass, with half a spoon of sugar.

When your order came, Nisnas brought out the red cellophane parcel and bit off a small piece, which he flattened on the back of the spoon and stirred into the tea. He patted you on the back once more. "Enjoy in good health. I'm sure you'll do us proud. You'll be kwice kiteer!"

But you signed that you didn't want it now. He bit off another piece and wrapped it in paper. "A present from me to you," he signed. "Put it under your tongue before you leave your room. It will keep you upright. Everything is in God's hands."

You raised your hands to your head to thank him, and savored the tea slowly, as you gazed from the gloom of the café out at the main road bustling with strange cars coming from north and south.

A little later you crossed the road, with your wedding gallabiya under your arm, your cropped hair no longer shielding you from the harshness of the burning sun. Your nose sniffed the powder that al-Adal had dusted on the back of your neck and the places where he had plucked out the fuzz with a thread gripped in his teeth. You felt as if your head weighed nothing at all. As usual, you pulled up the collar of your gallabiya and sank your scrawny head between your shoulders. You walked along without lifting your eyes from the ground, ignoring everybody, though they didn't want to ignore you. They came rushing up, they clung on, they wanted to stand and talk, purely for entertainment and fun.

Finally you came to the shop window, where the customers stood to collect their orders. You disappeared among the hanging remains of the carcass, and signaled to Zaki. He didn't notice you, but you were surprised to find Ammour approaching, gesturing to you. "Come on in. The maallim's inside with the shaykh."

You pulled your hand away from him, but he yanked you inside, pushing you down the two steps. The shaykh signed, "Come here."

You approached, embarrassed and hesitant. The maallim signed, "You're off work today."

You replied that you knew, but that you didn't know what to do with your long day.

"That's no excuse," the shaykh replied. "You're just dying to know if the promise will be kept." He leaned over to whisper something in the maallim's ear, and the maallim stretched behind him to open a drawer and pull out a large key. He called to Ammour and said, "Take him and show him the room, then call in at the shoe shop and let him choose a new pair of shoes."

Then he smiled at you and signed, "Shoes to crack your skull with."

The shaykh roared with laughter and said, "His bride will do that for him, God willing!"

You walked with Ammour along the busy Agriculture Street, avoiding the greetings of the shop owners and lowering your gaze from anyone you knew, so no one could hold you up. Ammour strode purposefully ahead of you, and turned off for the shoe shop. He said to the owner, "Where's the maallim's order?"

The man bent over behind the counter. "It's ready."

He lifted up a cardboard box, and took a pair of brown shoes from it. "They're exactly your size," he signed to you. "Or would you rather try them on?"

You took off one of your old leather slippers and inserted your foot into the shoe, squeezing it in with difficulty. You stamped hard on the ground, and your foot settled in comfortably. You signed to the man that the fit was just right, and he signaled his congratulations. He gave you a large bag, and you put the gallabiya and the shoe box into it together, making your load easier. You carried it carefully and plunged back into the crowds of people, until you entered a side street to join a quiet road on which just one or two cars passed occasionally. Then

96

you crossed it again to a road that took you out into the broad green fields.

This was your daily route to the maallim's house, which you were no longer allowed to visit, though you didn't know why. The smell of manure from the byre mixed with the breath of the animals hit your nostrils, and you raised your head to see her beautiful face looking down from the balcony.

She was wringing the washing and hanging it out on the lines. She ignored your gaze, as well as your greeting. Even when you repeated your greeting, she didn't turn toward you at all, and you yelled, "Ab . . . ab," and shook your hand at the side of your head. She recoiled at your shout and spat angrily on the ground, before raising her hand to her luminous neck to make a cutting motion with it several times, meaning she would slit your throat.

—So, she doesn't want to say hello, and she doesn't want me to attract attention to her on the balcony.

Ammour pulled you through the broad byre and up some narrow stairs to a single room on the roof that still gave off a strong and penetrating smell of limewash paint. "Now are you happy, mate?" he signed to you. "A room and all its furnishings."

You opened the door to see a bed with tall, black posts and new sheets, a wardrobe whose glossy wood shone when you lit the lamp suspended from the ceiling, a wide sofa with pieces of old rug on it, and a new mat spread in the middle of the room. From under the bed, Ammour pulled some boxes full of eating utensils, pans, dishes, a primus stove, tea glasses, and coffee cups. "The maallim is a generous man," he signed. "He gave up his mother's furniture and renovated it. And he said in front of me"—he pointed to his eyes—"the boy's worth it."

You stepped back. You didn't know whether to be happy or upset. Were you expecting more than this? Think yourself lucky: you're starting from nothing, you've never saved a millieme all your life. And the man's been good to you—he's asked nothing of you, he hasn't even hinted he'll take anything out of your wages.

So let it be a beginning with your new bride. Through hard work, and sweat, and adding piaster to piaster, you can improve your situation. Your life is ahead of you. It's enough that you're going to live your own married life, and leave your brother's world and get out from under his control. Here, you will be the master of the house.

—Certainly, the room isn't up to the standard I was hoping for. But never mind, I'll make do with a little, and I'll make this the start of a new life.

You turned and followed Ammour down the stairs. He was in a hurry. On the way, he signaled to you with his bunched fingers to his mouth, kissing them: "What could be better than that?"

You nodded your head submissively, and pushed him in the direction of the crowded Agriculture Street, while you made your way back to your neighborhood along the quiet road.

Anxiety gnawing at your heart, you wondered, "Why did she act so strangely? Why did she spit in my face, and make the throat-slitting gesture? Did I do something to upset her?"

You turned your head back and looked up to see the washing there, but she had disappeared behind the closed balcony door.

2

The heavy knocking at the door woke him. He left behind the creatures he had been sporting with and opened his eyelids to see the pictures of Suad Hosni, Hasan Yusuf, Shukri Sarhan, and Hind Rustum, and the many pictures of foreign actors and actresses, headed by Marilyn Monroe, Sophia Loren, and Cary Grant, all of them in bathing costumes that revealed more than they concealed—color photographs illuminated by the pale light falling through the glass of the north-facing window.

The faces of sleep were quickly obliterated, and the other faces were affirmed—faces that he loved but most of whose owners he did not know, as he had cut them at random from *The Stars* and *The Final Hour*.

He always forgot his dreams quickly. The only ones that stayed with him were the nightmares that took hold of his throat and forced him to wake up in order to escape the cruel grasp that throttled him. For a while he would remain paralyzed, unable to move, his tongue cleaved to the roof of his mouth so that he could not scream or cry for help. And who would help him in that silent house? His mother had left for work, and he was condemned to solitude.

Moments of pleasure were ignited at weddings, among people, when his voice rang out with "Bid Your Love Farewell," "My Sweetheart's Eyes," or "My Heart Is Fond of You" into a microphone that amplified it tenfold through huge speakers broadcasting to all corners of the tent.

The knocking came again, this time on the windowpane. He heard a voice surprised at the lack of response. "Even a corpse would have woken up."

"Who's there?"

"Man, the day's over."

"Who is it?"

"It's me, Ammour."

"Ammour who?"

"Open up, and I'll tell you."

He got up, pulled together his unbuttoned pajamas, combed his fingers through his soft hair, rubbed his face with his hands, and yawned lazily. He stretched his body to left and right, then looked for his slippers beside the bed and put them on the wrong feet. The knocking started again.

"Hold on."

"God give me patience."

He changed feet in his slippers and felt much better. He wanted to let out a fart, but refrained for fear of being heard outside. He opened the front door. The yellow light hurt his eyes, so he put up his hand to shield them. "Yes? Who are you, sir?"

"Sir is Ammour, who works for Maallim Osman."

Now that his eyes had grown accustomed to the soft afternoon light, he looked him up and down. He was shocked by the blood spattered on the filthy white gallabiya, the knives tucked into the belt, and the smell of rotten meat that wafted in with the afternoon breeze. "Move away a bit."

"Move away where? I've come to tell you a couple of things, and then I'm out of here."

He stood ready to receive the couple of things, pinching his nose between two fingers and averting his eyes from the man's ironical expression, focusing on the weak yellow light that fell on the façades of the houses opposite.

"There's no need for all that."

"Get to the point, or I'll leave you standing here and go back inside."

"Maallim Osman says everything's ready at the Lulu hairdressing salon."

"Fine. Okay."

"The groom will come and collect your highness there. The whole gang will be there. And don't let the cat out of the bag."

"I know."

"You take care of yourself now, miss—I mean, sir."

"Go to blazes!" And he slammed the door in his face.

The man's laughter came to him through the peep window, and he only regained his composure when the odious shadow had disappeared from the glass.

Now he could relieve his stomach of its gasses without heed, but even so when he went into the bathroom he first stood in front of the basin to gaze at his face in the mirror, feeling his cheeks with his delicate fingers. He scooped up the water in his hands and splashed it on his face, poked a finger in each ear, turned back his lips to look at his shining white teeth, pressed on his upper gum, then his lower gum, took a handful of water to gargle, brushed his teeth up and down and back again, spat the water out into the basin, and went back to gargling once more. He picked up the comb and passed it through his hair to flatten it to one side. First he combed it back, then to the right, then flat down again, and finally set it in place to the left as usual. Then he removed his pajama trousers and his smalls and hung them on the hook, and squatted over the hole to empty his churning and painful bowels. He washed himself well, and dried his nether parts with a handkerchief. He took off the rest of his clothes to prepare for the cold water of the shower, soaped up the loofah, and washed under his arms, between his thighs, and between his buttocks with it. Then he scrubbed his ears and his neck, taking care not to wet his hair, so that he would be able to leave the house quickly. He reached for the black stone to clean his heels, and ran the perfumed soap between his toes. He let the water pour over his white, hairless body, then yanked at the bath towel to dry himself all over with its ends, before wrapping it around his waist and once more staring at his face in the mirror. He felt relaxed and fit.

In the hallway he found the tray his mother had laid out for him with his daily meal, and he lifted off the white towel. He dipped a piece of bread in the honey, and another in the cheese, then picked a black olive in his fingers and bit deliberately into its flesh.

This was how his mother left him every day when she had finished her housework and carried the barrels to the bouza shop to prepare that evening's drink. They met only fleetingly when he returned late from a wedding, or when he was able to spend some time with her customers on the days when he did not have work. There was one month in the year that brought them together, and caused them to spend long stretches in each other's company at home: Ramadan, the month of no bouza and no weddings. She would hug him to her, and he would stretch out with his head on her lap as she played with his soft hair and told him stories of his father and his grandmother or indulged in her dreams of what she wished for him before the end of her days. She would bend over every now and then to kiss his forehead, and he would grasp her hand and kiss it fondly. It was this hand that he would feel, when fast asleep, stroking his face with a sigh, wiping the sweat away, straightening the hair that fell over his brow. And between waking and sleep, he would be aware of the presence that came near to kiss his eyelids that were closed over wonderful pictures, bursting with screaming colors and illuminated by a bright light from somewhere that made the sequins shimmer on the dancing girls' dresses and the drops of sweat shine on the exposed flesh. Living bodies that shake on the raised boards in answer to the crazed rhythms of a band whose faces dissolve in the diaphanous veil of hashish smoke and dust raised by the feet of the guests who, also responding to the rhythm, swing and shake and throw largesse under the dancers' feet.

He approached the large, clear mirror of his room, having switched on the ceiling light, and continued examining his face, looking for the fine fluff on his ears and cheeks. The growth of small hairs like these annoyed him. He could not bear to see a hair on his body, and he was engaged in a constant struggle against every hair that poked its head out of a pore on his skin. He would treat them with sugar and lemon juice, patiently pursuing the dark spots scattered on his chest, his legs, or his arms.

He caught sight of Suad Hosni exchanging a cheeky smile with Sophia Loren in the mirror, and he turned around to see the original. How he longed to be an actor. He had taken small parts in school plays, silly roles that did not show off his real potential. The performances were tied to celebrations of national events, and the words he was made to memorize were meaningless. He came to hate school, as he hated its curriculum, its depressing formal celebrations, and its teachers who pretended gravity and carried on their shoulders the burden of disciplining humankind. They walked through the streets or within the school walls like high priests, carrying their canes under their arms ready to tan hides, with or without reason.

He would never forget that teacher (perhaps he taught Arabic or religion, or both) who sat him on a chair, stretched his bound legs out in front of him, and called the janitor to hold his head at one end while he gripped his legs at the other—and oh! how he dealt those blows. Why? What sin had the boy committed, his colleagues asked him? The teacher did not answer, but only shouted, "He knows the reason!"

Even now Hamada could not understand what had motivated the teacher. All that happened was that he had seen him with another boy under the stairs, away from the other boys' play in the long, tedious break period. They were showing each other their little members. The other boy lay on his back, while Hamada lifted the boy's tunic, pulled down his trousers, and leaned over to look at his willy. Did it look like the thing he had, or was it different? He found he had a desire to lick it with his tongue, but suddenly a rough hand picked him up by the scruff of the neck, threw him down on the tiles, then dragged him off to the teachers' room. The other boy jumped quickly to his feet, hurriedly pulling up the trousers around his ankles. The teacher slammed Hamada to the floor and yelled in his face, "Wait until the break is over so that your punishment can be in front of all the teachers!"

He lost nothing by leaving the school. He went out to a liberated life. It was enough that he had learned to unravel the alphabet and read words, which allowed him to collect the magazines that gave him the news of the stars, and to write to the addresses published for the fans. Suad Hosni was the first to reply. She wrote:

Mr. Hamada,
I love you just as much as you love me, and I hope to see you soon in the film studios fulfilling your ambition to be a famous star. This is not impossible, as you believe. On the contrary, it is an easy matter if you are truly gifted.

But his mother had refused to let him leave her, leave the town. "How can you abandon me here on my own? You're the apple of my eye."

—So here's an opportunity to bring out my talent. Let it be a first try. Yes, I'll be playing a woman, but why not? All the great actors played this sort of role, even the ones who weren't blessed with beauty or good looks. Ali al-Kassar did it, for example. Ismail Yassin did it. Why shouldn't I, since I have the beauty? When Munim puts a bit of make-up on me I'll be a true bride. And nobody in the town will discover who I really am. I hope the maal-lim and the shaykh have kept the secret well enough for me to give a great performance.

He took off the towel and walked naked across the room to fetch his case from the wardrobe, open it, and extract the see-through women's garments. He donned the red slip and panties, wrapped the bra and stockings in a bundle to take with him, hung the gold chain around his neck, and finished dressing by putting on his regular shirt and trousers.

—No need for anything else. Munim must have a full make-up set.

He bent over at the open door of the wardrobe, took out a pair of high-heeled women's shoes, and put them in a plastic bag along with the bra and stockings. He went into the hall, took a drink from the water jar with the sprig of basil tied around its neck, and went out into the street. The shadows had taken total possession of all the walls, and nothing was left of the sun but small patches of light that caught the piles of kindling on the roofs and the edges of the grain stores and pigeon lofts.

He was appalled by the crowds at Munim's salon when he neared it. The young men rushed toward him and hoisted him onto their shoulders, chanting "Hamada! Hamada!" He struggled to get away, kicking angrily at them with his feet. "Put me down!" But they were determined to carry him right up to the raised platform in front of the salon. Munim came out to calm him. In his great fury he cursed everybody, in particular the maallim and the shaykh.

"What did you expect?" Munim asked him. "The whole town knows, with one exception."

"And what's it all for?"

"That's how the maallim wants it."

"I'm not playing any more."

"For shame! You've taken a down payment."

"I don't care. With bells on."

He tried to jump down from the platform, but they held onto him from all sides and lifted him up again. "You have to see it through to the end," they said with one voice.

"And what's it to do with you lot?"

"We want to watch."

"Well, get out of my light now, until Munim finishes his work." Cheers went up from the jostling crowd.

"We won't leave here until the groom comes. Then we'll take you on a grand procession around the town."

"Oh, hell."

Munim pulled him by the hand into the cool salon and let down the colored bead curtain.

"Have a seat." He pointed to the big chair, pushed Hamada's head under the tap, and began to shampoo his hair. Then he dried it with a towel, before putting him under the hairdryer. He called to his assistant and nodded, and the boy pulled up the thick maroon curtain and took out the flowing white wedding dress. He spread it out on his arms and said, "What do you think?"

"I was quite happy to do this, but that mob out there has paralyzed me."

"You'll be all right. Try to forget them, and concentrate on the role."

"But they're such brutes. Can you hear their crude talk?"

"Forget it, and give me your face. I'll paint your face into a picture like no one's seen before."

Hamada surrendered to the hairdresser's hand. He was now completely relaxed. Outside, the crowd multiplied as the evening advanced.

Munim turned on all the lights, and they heard a shout go up outside as the sound of car horns came from a distance: *beep beep bib-bib-beep!*

Engines roared, and voices soared. "He's going to dip his wick! He's going to dip his wick!" The bead curtain rose, and the maallim and the shaykh peered in at them. The shaykh approached the chair and took a good look at the face close up. "God bless the Perfection of Light! May I ask your hand for my Beloved Prophet?"

Hamada pushed at him coquettishly. The maallim's face lit up with a delighted smile, and he congratulated Munim on his handiwork. Then he went up to Hamada and mockingly offered him the traditional greeting after somebody has had a haircut.

"Is the groom with you?" Hamada asked.

"Why are you in such a hurry, gorgeous?" said the shaykh, as he leaned over to give him a kiss on the cheek.

The maallim answered his question. "We came to check first. We're going to send the car to fetch him."

"What's the program, ya maallim?"

"There's no program or anything—just a bit of fun."

The shaykh stepped in to explain the plan in full to Hamada. "The groom will take you from here, and there'll be a procession all around the town—care of the lads outside. Then there's the apparent signing of the register—you know, not for real—in the tent pitched near the byre. Then a bit of singing and dancing until we've worn you both out, so that you won't be up to doing anything."

"There was nothing in our agreement about doing anything."

"I want him to get a shock when you reveal yourself."

"And who's going to protect me, ya maallim?"

"Do you think we're going to leave you alone? Heaven forfend! We'll all be around you."

"He might have a jack-knife, or a kitchen knife, or some other sharp tool."

"He's only got one tool, and he can't hurt you with that!" The shaykh's witticism had everyone roaring with laughter.

The crowd started chanting again, so the maallim went out to reassure them. "Everything in good time." He signaled to the car decorated with colored paper to go and fetch the groom, and went back into the salon. "Amazing. It's standing room only out there."

"And that's just the beginning," replied the shaykh.

3

When Agriculture Street had quietened down and hardly anyone was about, when customers had become very precious, Maallim Osman took out the day's takings and sorted the money piaster by piaster, placing all like notes together in one bundle and arranging all the bundles in the thick-doored iron safe. He looked around at his men and saw them standing among what was left of the hanging meat with nothing to do, so he issued the order to close the shop. He took Zaki to one side. "I want you to stand firm."

"Your secret's safe."

"I know he's your brother, and you're fond of him, so you might take pity on him."

"He's your man too, ya maallim."

"I want to teach him a lesson he won't forget."

"Whatever you say."

"Don't cave in. He asked for it."

"I'll do as you say, ya maallim."

"Go and clean yourself up, and come and join us there for the rest of the evening." And he guided him by the shoulder out of the shop.

Shaykh Saadoun stood up and stretched his fat body to the right and to the left, lifting his hands to his turban as opened his mouth wide in a long yawn. "I must have been asleep without realizing it."

"They could hear you snoring at the other end of the street."

"So why didn't you wake me up?"

"You have a long night ahead of you. I thought I'd let you get some sleep."

Shaykh Saadoun could set himself down anywhere, stop talking, lean his head on his hand, and fall asleep in no time. He would let out a snore powered by two broad, strong lungs, then suddenly wake up, wipe away his slobber with the palm of his hand, roll his eyes, and shout "Hayyy! Qayyum!" Then he would return to his slumber as though nothing had happened.

The maallim inserted his arm under the shaykh's arm, and led him outside, stepping off the curb onto the street. The shaykh then walked wearily behind him, clutching the edges of his quftan in his fingers, rather wishing he could go back to his bed for a real sleep, and succumbing every now and then to an extended yawn that forced his jaws so wide apart that it hurt.

Zaki went home dejected and defeated. Intoxication gives way to sober reality. How are you going to face people, ya Zaki? Colluding against your own brother?

—The maallim was perfectly clear: it's a matter of livelihood. I don't know any other trade, and even my evening job selling liver depends on the morning job.

His face cast down to the ground, he saw nothing around him. He felt the eyes of the remaining store owners following him, and sensed their astonishment at his lack of greeting as he passed.

—I wish the ground would swallow me up, tonight of all nights.

"Hey, dreamer!" shouted Disouqi the salted fish merchant from behind his marble counter.

He tossed his hand in the air, without making any verbal reply.

—Does Houda deserve such a punishment? The maallim didn't tell me what Houda did, or why he was angry with him.

When I asked him, he was curt: "He knows what he did, and he'll know even better when he gets a taste of what I've got planned for him on his wedding night."

—My brother. Son of my mother and father. This is the first time I've really felt that you're mute, that you can't speak. I never realized before that you were in any way deficient. And this is the first time too I've really felt that you're deaf, that you can't hear. I've lived with you all my life, and I treat you like anybody with all their senses. Clever. Perceptive. In fact cleverer and more perceptive than most people who can speak and hear. But the whole town knows one thing you don't know, and everyone's happy to watch, as if all of them had their own separate score to settle with you. Is it because you know more about them than you should?

He arrived at the station platform, which was empty of travelers. He lifted his head, happy to be walking in a quiet place, with nobody about. The sun's disc shone on him, red and sinking behind the high buildings to be swallowed by the fronds of the palms and the plants of the fields that stretched between the river and the railway line.

He passed by Mitwalli's café, where Aziza was fetching the empty chairs in from the sidewalk and Mitwalli was inside collecting the café equipment up in a palm basket.

"Where are you off to?"

"The whole town's over there, so we thought we'd set up a stall and make something out of the evening."

"Do you want your things?" Aziza asked him. Then she realized, and said, "Oh, of course, you're the brother of the groom! No liver tonight."

Zaki shook his head regretfully, and Mitwalli said, "Would you like some tea? There's just a drop left in the pot, but it's good and strong."

111

He left them packing up their things, and went off, avoiding the speeding cars, to turn down into the sloping street, which made him lean back and feel the pressure of his body on his thin legs. He saw the neighbors hurrying in his direction. They looked at him in astonishment. "The brother of the groom and you're not dressed yet?"

The women were all dolled up. They had lined their eyes with kohl, pinched their cheeks to bring the color to their faces, splashed cheap scent on their bodies, and put on their best dresses. They had also bathed the children, who wore their festival clothes and were being either dragged by the hand or carried in their mothers' arms, as innocently happy as could be. The women pushed on up the street toward the tent, whose lights would illuminate a party that might well go on until morning.

He ignored them, as he ignored what they said about him still being in the neighborhood, which seemed to annoy them.

He saw the owner of the cheese factory sitting on his chair on the sidewalk with his legs crossed, amazed by what he saw. He sucked in his lips and said to Zaki, "Look what the world's come to: the women have lost their marbles."

"It looks like the town's choking for any kind of party."

"As long as it doesn't affect business. Who's going to milk the animals tonight? Are they leaving it to their menfolk, or should I shut up shop and go home?"

"You only think of yourself," Zaki said under his breath, and he left him and walked alongside the wall of the big house. The sparrows were collecting in the mulberry trees as night fell, twittering clamorously, each one searching out its roost after filling its belly with the blessings of the earth. He did not know whether their din was a celebration of the rest earned with the long night, or a lament for the passing day.

He collided with Aida, coming out of the door in a line with her sisters. She felt his chest with her hands, then said angrily, "Zaki! What are you doing here?"

At the end of the line, her mother said, "Shouldn't you be over there? It's your brother's wedding."

"The maallim and his men are taking care of it. I'm going to have a wash, and I'll see you there."

Aida thought it a good opportunity to ask, "Has the maallim really slaughtered a steer?"

"You know," Nawal added, "everybody's saying he's going to give a kilo of raw meat to everyone in town." Her sister hit her with the empty aluminum pan to encourage her to move on, so that she could pick up her share before the crowds arrived.

Since Zaki had not given an answer, Umm Ali repeated the question. "Has he really slaughtered?"

"Maybe he'll take the meat from the shop."

"Well, it's all meat anyway."

He heard the voice of the Azhar student, who had attached himself to the line. "They say he's brought a leading chef from Cairo." He was leaning over his crippled leg, raising his head toward Zaki, anticipating a reply.

He passed through the door, allowing the line to proceed. The Azhar student dragged his leg, and the soft dust rose around him. Zaki waved his hand in front of his face to clear away the dust, and he coughed vigorously until the phlegm reached his mouth. He spat it onto the ground and trod it in.

"The fool eats at the madman's table."

He went into the room, where his brother was hidden behind the sheet hung over the rope, scooping water in a jug from a pan from which a light steam rose. He was standing naked in the shallow tub, unaware of anything around him, trying to rinse the suds from his face. Zaki heaved a deep sigh, and despite trying to contain his feelings, he heard his voice come out: "Oh, my dear brother!"

He looked at him over the sheet and smiled. Having cleaned away the soap, Houda now opened his happy eyes and signed to Zaki, "May your wedding bath be soon."

He collapsed and stretched out on the mat, staring at the ceiling. He almost surrendered to the slumber that was gathering the fragments of his exhausted energies, but he was roused by his brother's voice. "Ab . . . ab . . . ." And Houda signed to him that there was water left that he could wash in. Zaki lifted his hand to his head and signed back, "I'll just change my clothes."

He took his clean gallabiya and spread it out in front of him, then took off his work clothes and splashed his face with the lukewarm water, drying it quickly. He inserted his head into the neck of the gallabiya, and without looking at his brother he signed to him, "I'll go on ahead. Don't leave the room—the car (he gripped an imaginary steering wheel with his hands) will pick you up from here and take you to the hairdresser's. That's where the bride is (he made hairdressers' scissors with his index fingerand second finger at his head)."

Houda made a last attempt to ask about the bride that the maallim had chosen, but Zaki avoided the question and left the room quickly.

4

The light outside took you by surprise. Was this the last time you would ever leave your dark room? It was a gloomy, gray light, with no sun to it—the remains of the wick of the lamp of the universe, which had been extinguished over there beyond the houses and the fields. In the weak light you could not see the hole of the lock, and your hand shook slightly as you fixed the clasp with it. Why was your hand shaking? Was it because you were leaving the place where you had spent your life with the brother who protected you and looked after you after your parents died? Perhaps. Or perhaps because you were about to enter an unprecedented and mysterious world of which you had no experience?

Why were you nervous about a day you had spent your life looking forward to? Was this not your life's dream, to leave this loathsome room? To live in a house all your own, with a wife who would bring you children to be your support in the future? Your dream had been made real. The maallim—God grant him a long life—had made everything easy for you. With his well-known sharpness of mind he had read the desires of your body, and made them come true, without asking you for a millieme. You were lucky to have him. He had picked you and your brother up from the street, found work for you in his shop, and now, at just the right time, he was giving you your marital home.

Were you afraid, then? Of what? Of the demands of this night, of what was said about the incompatibility of some couples on their first encounter, particularly as you had been presenting your-self as a wire about to snap? No, that was not frightening at all—plenty of men had been through it before, and their lives had gone on and they joked about it among themselves. And, thank goodness, no one had raised any doubts about your own compati-bility. No one would be with you—she and you would be alone together in the room after the partying was over. And if your body didn't rise to the occasion tonight, you could put it off until tomorrow or the day after.

Would she have family asking after her? Who was her mother? Her father? Her brother? This was the nub of the matter, and one of the real reasons for your nervous state: Who was the bride? If you knew her already, it would all be less disturbing.

—Well, whoever she is, she's a woman like any other woman.

You had convinced yourself before that the maallim was a man of experience when it came to women, and when he selected someone for one of his men, he would choose a woman suitable in both beauty and manners. It was in his own interests, so that the man would remain beholden to him his whole life.

Perhaps it was one of the servant women who came to the shop, or a poor girl, the daughter of a good man who had once worked for him, or the daughter of one of the men working at the byre.

—Anyway, whoever she is, in the end she's a woman like any other woman. And I'm a man like any other man. When the door of our room closes behind us, we'll have other concerns. This mar-riage goes back to the old days, the days of our fathers and mothers, when no man saw his future bride in advance. She would be revealed to him on the wedding night, and it was a matter of luck—either one of the gardens of paradise or one of the pits of hell. Or, it was like a watermelon, also a matter of luck—whether it would be red or white inside, only God knew. These days, watermelons are split open before you buy them, so why can't you do it the modern way, ya maallim? Then I would be able to approach her more calmly, with a quieter heart. But as it is, my situation would suit neither friend nor foe: I'm going in blind.

—I wonder if she knows who I am? Have they told her the name of the husband she'll wait for alone in the room? Has she heard the name of the man who'll throw himself into her embrace tonight? The man who'll break the secret seal and penetrate its hidden depths? She must have a mother who's told her, or a father who agreed to the marriage. And surely she has a working pair of ears and could hear it from a sister, a neighbor, a relative? When they mention my name, she'll know it. But how am I supposed to know who she is? By sign language? That isn't enough to distinguish one woman out of the thousands in this place. She would have to be very close to my world, then I would easily be able to tell who she is from the first sign about her face, her walk, the build of her body—any sign, I'll get it quickly and know who's being referred to.

The further people were from your limited circle, the harder it was to define them in sign language, unless they were very well known or had some distinguishing feature not shared by anybody else.

Anyway, you had prepared yourself well for your big night. A good haircut and shave, on which al-Adal had taken sufficient time and worked diligently and devotedly. You had impressed upon him that a haircut for a casual customer was not the same as one for a bridegroom. He also worked on your face with the thread held between his teeth to remove all the light fuzz, so that your cheeks became smooth and pleasant to touch. Then a warm bath to open the pores, scrubbing well with the loofah and scented soap under your arms, where you had removed the sweaty hair. You also scrubbed well between your legs, after pruning your

117

pubic hair with a pair of rusty iron scissors—whose points kept escaping your control, almost doing you an injury in a sensitive part of your body and severing all joy from tonight's proceedings. Luckily, you were miraculously spared, and you then took the uncooperative scissors to your fingernails and clipped them evenly. Then you scrubbed the backs of your hands with the loofah until they were suffused with blood. From the bottle you kept concealed among your folded clothes you splashed scent on your chest, under your arms, around your neck, and on the hairs of the moustache that you had trimmed in the mirror by the fading light that squeezed through the window. And now here you were inserting your clean body, after drying it thoroughly, into new underwear that smelled pleasantly of cotton. Your skin relaxed to the touch of the undershirt and undertrousers. You put your head through the neck of the new, white gallabiya, extended your arms into the sleeves, and pulled it down. You did all this carefully, mindful of the ironing and not wanting the garment to acquire any creases before the bride's eyes fell on it and before the people could admire it when they caught sight of you, the star of the evening.

You put your feet into the new shoes. No need for socks, as the shoes were tight enough, and you had to force your feet into them. The leather was stiff and hard, and you stamped on the ground a couple of times until your heels dropped in. You walked around the room in the shoes, skirting the tub, stepping warily on the mud, and scuffing the smooth soles on the floor to roughen them so that you would not slip and fall.

Now you were outside your room, standing hesitantly in the long hall to wait for the car that would carry you to your bride, and to your new home. You stood at the main door and peered out cautiously, and were surprised at how still the street was. Where had everybody gone? There were no women over there under the acacia

tree, no children playing in front of the houses, no animals returning with their owners from the fields. It was totally quiet. It was
frightening. It was like the eternal silence of the big house, hidden
behind the dense mulberry trees where swarms of sparrows returned
to their roosts. The gloom deepened behind and all around.

He had never seen anyone leaving that house, or entering it. He
had never in his life seen a door open or a window ajar. When he
asked Zaki about the owners of the house, he signed to him that
they had left it for cities far away, some of them even going
abroad. Only a gaunt old woman lived there now, with a servant
woman just as old who called at the shop for a kilo of meat once
a week. Houda signed that he did not know her, and Zaki replied,
"I'll point her out to you when she comes in one day. The maallim
makes a great fuss of her, and gets up from his desk to cut the
meat for her himself."

Houda nodded and pointed a finger to his head to show that he
understood.

The sight of the house constricted the spirit and shrank the
soul. He imagined that ghosts looked down on him from behind
the trees. He turned his gaze in the opposite direction, but he was
drawn back to it, defeated and oppressed.

Would he have to wait long? They had told him, "Stay there
until the car comes to pick you up."

Why were they so late? He had locked the room, and now he
stood staring at the street, utterly bored. There was nobody to
help him pass the time. He had thought he would catch the
women gathered under the acacia tree, have fun with them, tease
them, answer their intrusive questions, put his hand out to this
one, flirt with that one, so that the heat would course through his
body, stimulating it, and . . . and . . . and what?

He would feast his eyes on Fakiha, and her exposed bosom. She sent all the devils of the land to his blood. Where was she now? Had she gone with the others to attend the wedding? Or would her hard-to-get attitude keep her from going? He hoped she would be there, so that she would be the last person he set his eyes on, and he could go in to his bride with inextinguishable passion.

He stepped back toward the entrance. Should he open the room again and crouch quietly and respectfully until they came for him? There was no one here. Even the Azhar student had gone with them—his large padlock hung on his door. And Umm Ali had certainly been taken along by her blind daughters, as this was an opportunity she would never miss.

He felt a hand touching his head. His hair stood on end, and his heart raced painfully. What was it?

My god, it was Fakiha, leaning out of the window of her room by the entrance. He screamed in surprise and fright, as he pointed to her and his heart, and the sound of his violent heartbeat came out of his mouth. He signed to her, "I almost died of shock."

Her face shining with white powder and intense red lipstick, she signed back, "Your poor heart."

He stood staring at the whiteness of her face, the loose, dark hair that fell around it, and the flirtatious, seductive smile that sent joy to his soul. She winked at him with her kohled lashes, and stirred her index finger in the open fist of her other hand: "Would you like some tea?"

He screeched in delight. "Ab . . . ab!"

He lifted the hem of his gallabiya and sprang through the open door and down the two steps into the dark hall. On the right were the stairs to Umm Ali's sitting room; under them lurked the toilet, with its battered old wooden door.

She opened the door of her room. He stood there flabbergasted, unable to lift his feet over the raised threshold. He was dazzled by that red dress with the soft fluff that descended from behind the head and extended over the bosom, leaving an area of light below the throat, above the heaving heights, and between the two tormenting breasts.

She held her hand out to him and signed, "Are you waiting for an invitation?"

He went in.

He remained silent, looking at the things in the room. The wardrobe with its one mirror. The clean bed with its folded covers. The sofa with its bright white mattress and backrests. The plastic mat spread between the sofa and the bed.

At one time, he had sat on this very mat, when it was brand new and the room had a smell of things not yet worn out. Fikri used to call him in to set up his goza for a couple of smokes. Fakiha would light the primus stove for them and arrange a row of corn cob kernels on it, which she then buried in the ashes of the brazier while she went off to see to the tea. Houda would set up a tobacco bowl, and Fikri would draw hard until the hashish on top of it glowed. He would throw glances at Fakiha, up on the sofa in all her splendor, busy embroidering her white headscarf with its bright flowers in screaming colors. He would glance and return to himself weary and sad. He envied his neighbor for owning all this enchantment.

He tried to make her look his way, but she tortured him and did not even peek at him, remaining engrossed in her handiwork, her eyelids lowered as she watched the needle between her long, white fingers. He would sigh, exhale the fire from his chest along with the smoke of the honey-tobacco, and go back to placing coals on the tobacco bowl. As he passed the reed to Fikri, his mouth emitted noises intended as the traditional greeting between hashish smokers.

More than once, while setting up the gozas at Mitwalli's café, he surreptitiously stripped the hashish with his tongue, to put together a reasonable piece to tempt his neighbor with when he met him in the evening. He would signal to him when he came home from work, "I've got a great piece of dope."

So Fikri would invite him in for an evening to which he had become addicted.

He tried—later—to keep the custom going, but Fikri signed to him that he had given up smoking hashish, making do with the occasional cigarette. He coughed roughly, spat out the phlegm, and gestured for Houda to understand that the doctor had ordered him to stop. So Houda had no more reason to visit him, and he was deprived of these pleasurable evenings.

Now here he was back there with her, without Fikri. He sniffed the mixed aromas of woman's scent, stale air, sweaty clothes, bedsheets, and wood covered in dust and damp.

He asked her where Fikri was, and she signed, "He's over there with the other guests, waiting for the groom—which is you."

He gave a perplexed laugh, as though he had forgotten all about that, forgotten he was the bridegroom tonight, forgotten all the preparations he had looked forward to. He felt as if he had lived in this room for a long time. He asked her, "Why didn't you go with him?"

She smiled, and signed back, "Go and wait for who? When the groom is here with me, alone?"

She sat next to him.

They were face to face.

She signed that she was going to tell him a secret, but that he must not get excited, and should remain calm so that no neighbor would hear them. This amazed him. What secret? Was she going to tell him that she loved him? Why hadn't this happened before? Why did she wait all this time to tell him her secret, on his wedding day? He placed his hand over his mouth, a sign that he would keep silent.

She told him the whole story of the maallim's hoax, as she ran her slender fingertips along the collar of the clean, white gallabiya.

His eyes glistened in the dark, and the tears almost flowed down his cheeks. He had never felt the knot that tied his tongue as much as he did at this moment. He wanted to erupt, to tear something apart, to put his bony fingers around someone's neck, someone unknown, someone whose features he could not make out, because he possessed more than one face. He wanted to squeeze that person's neck with these fingers until his head lolled on his chest. He wanted to yell, to scream. Or to burst apart all over the room.

But she kept him completely under her control. She kept her eyes on his, in a steady gaze that held him still. He stared into space, his eyes wide, containing the emptiness of the room. She raised her hand to seal his mouth. Then she lifted it to play with the hairs of his moustache, and brought her other hand up to his ear. He surrendered to her completely.

He wanted to ask her how she knew about it. He could not stop the strangled rattle in his throat, and she relieved him of having to ask the question, which she knew. She signed that the maallim had summoned Fikri to paint the bridal room, so he had come to know the whole story.

He signed with a heavy hand, "Does anybody else know?"

In reply, she swept both arms around her in the air to indicate that the whole town knew.

He brought his two index fingers together: "And does Zaki know?"

She stood up to her full height in front of him. "The first to know."

He pronounced the "Oh!" like any person with a voice.

He wrapped his arms around her waist, and laid his face on the taut dome of her abdomen. She ran her fingers through his hair, rocking him and holding him to her in a light, gentle embrace. He buried his face in her belly, plunging into it like a fugitive, wanting to disappear, wanting to melt away in her blood, leaving behind the world around him.

His own blood moved again in his veins, and the keenness of the calamity gradually eased. He was pleased to find that he could rise steadily to his feet, and he stood in front of her. Face met face, eye met eye. Then, finally, mouth met mouth.

His strength had returned, and he was able to push her back and climb with her onto the bed. She submitted tenderly, and made her own demands.

He was astonished to find himself standing in front of her completely naked, having stripped off all the new clothes from his body, which he now launched at her. She received him with a welcome that brought him into intimacy and empathy, toward her surging sea of compassion.

5

This was the second time he had come back. The first time, the maallim had said to him furiously, "You'd better dive down and come up with your brother from the depths of the earth."

The cars had returned empty, and they had told him they had not found the groom in his room, which was bolted and locked. The whole house was empty, there was no one there, either upstairs or downstairs. They had tried to find a neighbor to ask, but there was nobody around at all.

The maallim shoved Zaki out. "Go, and don't come back without him."

He did not believe that anyone in the town could have leaked the secret to Houda. Everybody was enjoying the game too much and wanted to see how it turned out. It was just not possible. Everyone had been guarding the flame—when would they ever see such fun as this? It was a once-in-a-lifetime occurrence.

Zaki crossed the road in a stupor. Where could Houda have gone?

—When I left him he was so excited. He was taking his bath, getting ready for his big night, hardly able to believe his good fortune. I gave him no hint of any kind. Could he have met someone on the way, who told him what was going on? On the way? But he wasn't going on foot. I told him, "Don't leave the room until the car comes to take you to the wedding." So he couldn't have left the house. Did someone take pity on him and sneak in to tell him the maallim's plan, and what the whole town had kept hidden from him?

He entered the dark passageway, where he could see nothing in front of his eyes. He lit a match and turned toward the room. The lock hung on the door. In the dark he called to him. "Houda! Ya Houda!"

No one answered. He called again. Umm Ali's head poked out of the upper window. "Open the door and see if he's inside."

His reply was disparaging. "How's he going to lock the door from the outside, do you suppose?"

The Azhar student came out in his underwear. "I came back and looked to see if he was here, but he wasn't. See if he's at Mitwalli's café."

"Mitwalli's closed." And he went back to tell the maallim what he had seen and what he had heard.

It was enough to make the maallim lose his self-control, and Shaykh Saadoun tried to calm him down. "Send your men out to look for him all over."

Maallim Osman screamed at the men standing around him, and they spread out in all directions to begin their search. But eventually they came back with no news. So then he gave the signal to take the whole show down. Hamada wiped the powder from his face, took off the wedding dress, and went home carrying his bag under his arm. The guests left.

The maallim stayed behind with Shaykh Saadoun, in front of Mitwalli's stall, the two of them rancorously puffing out the smoke of the goza. When the hashish had filled his head, and he was stoned enough to reach his own magical and captivating worlds, he smiled, then laughed out loud, then leaned back and clapped one hand against the other. Shaykh Saadoun joined him in his hilarity, and the infection of laughter spread to everyone else. The maallim wiped his face with his large handkerchief and said in wonder, "The boy's just dissolved away like a piece of salt."

"He's brighter than we thought he was."

The maallim expelled the smoke from his lungs. "We said he was mute and can't speak, deaf and can't hear, so we thought we could keep a lid on it."

"Maybe the lad just had wedding night nerves and took to his heels," suggested the shaykh.

The suppressed rage came back to gnaw at the maallim's heart, and he said, "The smart aleck thinks he can put one over on his betters! Where's he going to go? Sooner or later he'll slink back like a dog."

"It's a two-sheep town," said Mitwalli, putting his mouth to the reed.

The maallim's face was glowing as he pointed to Aziza lying beside her husband, exhausted from the day's work, "Okay, friend, gather up your sheep and clear out."

Zaki entered the room with his hands outstretched, looking for the kerosene lamp. He lit a match, and his few possessions showed up on the table blackened with dust and oil.

As he lit the wick of the lamp, things became clearer. The tub was still in its place, with the bathwater in it, and surrounded by a ring of mud. Houda's old shoes were on the floor next to the brush, and his filthy clothes were hung up on a nail. The towel was still wet. His nose caught the remnants of the scent, blended with their own breath that never left the room.

He shut the door behind him, but did not lock it from the inside.

—Perhaps he'll come back and want to get in without making any noise to wake me. But I'll sense him, however much he tries to hide. I'll smell his breath, I'll hear his breathing. Where are you now, ya Houda? Come back, and let whatever happens happen.

He lay his exhausted body down on the bed, resting his head on his hand. He lowered the wick of the lamp and the shadows took over, tall and spectral. For a long time he stared at the window open onto the street.

But the only thing he heard was Blind Amin's voice ringing out in the silence of the neighborhood. "Praised be He Who was named before He was named. Praised be He Who taught Adam the names of things."

He rose from his bed and stretched his body, pushing his arms out to front and back. He yawned as he called to his brother, "Houda. Wake up, ya Houda." But no one answered. The events of the night before went through his mind, and he felt a lump in his throat. He blew out the feeble little flame, and went outside alone. He walked silently in the silent street. He looked behind, hoping to see Houda walking toward him, and he turned his head right and left, but saw no one.

He waved good morning to Abu Sinna, stacking his crates outside his house, and watched the mother chasing her daughter with the broom. He smiled, threw a meaningful look to his left, and dug Houda in the ribs—but there was only empty air. He saw the women carrying the milk pots on their way to the cheese factory. They left their footprints in the dust as they trod on the light covering of dew. Everything went on as normal. It was as if these people had had no part in yesterday's game.

The main street was busy with cars. Mitwalli stood in front of the fire, burying the iron rod in it and taking it out red hot to cleanse the gozas. His wife was at the counter, watching the kettles on the sand box and pressing honey-tobacco into the bowls.

"Hasn't he shown up yet?"

"No."

"Where's he gone, then?"

"God knows."

He stood at the beginning of the bridge, where the crossing gates were, looking out for the arrival of the cart. Eventually he saw it coming, with the men pushing it from behind to help the donkey pull it up the steep incline. Once it reached the level road, they arranged themselves around its wooden boards, their legs dangling down on both sides, leaving room for the tubs and the butchering equipment.

Mechanically, as he was accustomed to, he jumped up onto the side of the cart, in his usual place. The driver gave rein to the donkey, which set off happily down to Market Street on its way to the abattoir.

Glossary

1967 war Better known internationally (but not in Egypt) as the Six Day War, this was the war in which Egypt lost Sinai to Israel.

Ali al-Kassar, Ismail Yassin Popular Egyptian film comedians of the mid-twentieth century. Al-Kassar often played the bumbling underdog. Yassin made a comic virtue out of his large mouth and rubber face. Both occasionally dressed in drag for comic effect.

al-Azhar University Cairo's ancient seat of religious learning, going back more than a thousand years.

bilela A sweet dish of stewed whole wheat, milk, and sugar.

bouza A fermented alcoholic beverage, thick and opaque, made from bread. Bouza is probably very similar to—and a descendent of—ancient Egyptian 'beer.'

Dayan General Moshe Dayan (1915–81) was the iconic face of the Israeli enemy for many Egyptians in the 1970s. The patch over his left eye makes him an easy mime for Houda.

evil eye Belief in the harm done by the evil eye, attracted by envy, is especially strong in rural Egypt. In Farha's case, it was assumed to be responsible for the deaths of all her previous children, hence the extra precautions taken to divert it from Hamada.

gallabiya A long garment worn, in different styles, by both men and women, especially in rural areas of Egypt.

goza A makeshift water pipe, usually put together from an old tin can or a glass jar and a piece of reed or cane, that is often favored by hard-worn hashish smokers. It works on the same principle as its more elaborate and elegant cousin the shisha. Honey-tobacco is placed in a small clay bowl, with a stone in its neck to stop the tobacco falling through the pipe that leads down into the water that half fills the tin can. Hashish can be placed on the tobacco, and hot coals are then placed on top of that. When the smoker draws on the reed stuck at an angle through the top of the can or jar, the smoke is drawn down from the bowl into the water, where it is cooled on its way up and eventually into the smoker's waiting lungs. The word goza literally means 'a nut,' because in the past the main component of the apparatus was often a coconut.

hagg The correct form of address for a man who has completed the pilgrimage to Mecca, though frequently used as a term of respect for any older man.

Hayy! Qayyum! Typical exclamations of a Sufi mystic, expressing an ecstatic love for God. They mean something like "Living!" and "Everlasting!" respectively.

henna Henna is a plant dye that turns the skin temporarily dark brown or red. Henna parties are often held before a wedding, and involve sex-segregated singing and dancing while henna is applied to the hands and sometimes also the feet.

kohl A black paste applied to the eyelids and lashes. Most often used by women in traditional society, it is also occasionally used by men, particularly those of a mystical inclination.

kwice kiteer British army pidgin Arabic, supposed to mean 'very good.' In the Arabic text at this point, Nisnas tells Houda he will be *bri-fiks*—an Egyptian corruption (probably also from the time of the British occupation) of 'perfect.'

maallim A designation and a term of respect for a businessman in traditional society who is of some standing but little or no formal education.

Mansoura, Sinbillawayn, Mit Ghamr, Tanta, Banha Towns of the eastern Nile Delta.

mawlana A respectful term of address for a shaykh.

millieme The smallest unit of Egyptian currency, one-tenth of a piaster, or one-thousandth of an Egyptian pound—effectively no longer in use.

mulid A celebration, often of several days' duration, centered around the 'birthday' of a revered holy figure at his or her tomb.

mulukhiya Jew's mallow *(Corchorus olitorius)*, the green leaves of which are used to make a popular Egyptian soup.

names While Houda, Zaki, Osman, Saadoun, Fikri, Radwan, Hamada, Mitwalli, Ammour, Umm Ali, Aida, Nawal, and Aziza are more or less common Egyptian names (Houda is a popular pet form of Mahmoud; Hamada likewise for Muhammad or sometimes Ahmad; and Ammour for Amr), some of the other names in this novel are unusual and deserve some explanation. Abu Sinna means 'he of the front tooth'—a nickname likely to be given to a man with a single tooth to his smile. Al-Adal is a nickname meaning 'muscles.' Al-Hosari, the family name of Shaykh Saadoun and Hagg Radwan, means, appropriately enough, 'the mat-maker.' Shams, who the maallim first remembers as shining like the morning sun, means . . . 'sun.' Fakiha comes from a root having to do with being cheerful or jocular. Farha means 'joy.' Kaka is a children's word that means 'pooh,' Nisnas means 'monkey,' and Qunsul means 'consul.'

osta A designation and a term of respect for a man in a skilled occupation, such as a builder or a mechanic.

Palestine War The first war with Israel, in 1948.

prayer bruise Many Muslim men develop a callus on their forehead from its contact with the ground in the prostrations of the five daily prayers. The "government" that Houda mimes with his reference to the prayer bruise is President Anwar Sadat (1970–81), under whose rule the novel is set, and who bore a prominent forehead callus.

Proclaim the unity of God! Although this phrase means exactly what it says—that is, it is an exhortation to pronounce one of the key tenets of Islam: "There is no god but God"—it is also frequently used to break a long silence, and is the functional equivalent of "Somebody say something!"

quftan A long garment often worn by shaykhs under a long open-fronted cloak.

Ramadan The month of the Islamic calendar devoted to fasting and pious pursuits. No weddings are held during Ramadan, and intoxicating drinks such as Farha's bouza cannot be served.

Setback, Crossing The disastrous 1967 war (see above) is often known as the Setback. The Crossing came six years later, in October 1973, when Egyptian forces crossed the Suez Canal and broke the supposedly impregnable Bar-Lev Line to regain part of Sinai. Although the reoccupation was only temporary, this was the psychological breakthrough the Egyptians needed, and it was the first step to the Camp David peace treaty of 1978 and the handover of all of Sinai between 1979 and 1989.

shaykh This title means different things in different parts of the Arab world. For Egyptians, it most commonly designates a man of formal religious learning or, as in the case of Shaykh Saadoun, informal mystical inclination.

"slaughter an animal already in its death throes" In Islam, meat is only *halal* (lawful) if the animal has been slaughtered with a knife and the correct pronouncements have been made. If it dies of natural causes or in an accident, its meat cannot be eaten and thus has no value—hence the anxiety of the farmers to have their animals slaughtered before they die.

Suad Hosni, Hasan Yusuf, Shukri Sarhan, Hind Rustum Iconic Egyptian big screen actors and actresses of the 1960s. Suad Hosni, who embodied innocent, girlish charm and cheek, was everybody's sweetheart, while Hind Rustum was made of hotter stuff and was commonly dubbed the Egyptian Marilyn Monroe. Shukri Sarhan was a handsome leading man, though he also took on more complex roles. Hasan Yusuf was occasionally a leading man, but more often played the leading man's best friend or the leading lady's brother.

zikr A rhythmic mystic dance often performed at mulids, the aim to approach closer to God through the holy aura of the revered figure around whom the mulid is based.

Passages from the Quran
An ant exclaimed: ... Surat al-Naml (27):18
And there came traffic, ... Surat Yusuf (12):19
Say: I seek refuge in the Lord of the daybreak ... Surat al-Falaq (113):1
Say: I seek refuge in the Lord of mankind, ... Surat al-Nas (114):1

Translator's Note

usuf Abu Rayya was born in 1955 in the eastern Nile Delta
town of Hihya, a small rural center rather like the unnamed
town of *Wedding Night*. After studying journalism and media sci-
ences at Cairo University, he embarked on a career in journalism
and writing that have led him to the respected position he enjoys
today. He has published six collections of short stories and five
novels (*'Atash al-sabbar* [Cactus Thirst], *Tall al-hawa* [Passion Hill],
al-Gazira al-bayda' [The White Island], *Laylat 'urs* [Wedding
Night], and *'Ashiq al-hayy* [The Lover]), and has also written seven
books for children, most recently *Mughamarat Marku Bulu* (The
Adventures of Marco Polo). So far, his only works to have
appeared in English translation have been two short stories:
"Dreams Seen by a Blind Boy," in *Arabic Short Stories* (London:
Quartet Books, 1983); and "Out in the Open," in *Under the Naked
Sky* (Cairo: The American University in Cairo Press, 2000), both
translated by Denys Johnson-Davies.

Wedding Night was the unanimous choice of the judges for the
2005 Naguib Mahfouz Medal for Literature. In their citation, they
employed phrases like "transgresses boundaries on many levels,"
"profound psychological, metaphysical, and social signification,"
"a true literary talent," "a sea of stories," "the rural counterpart to
Mahfouz's critical dissection of the urban world," "a literary legacy
that Yusuf Abu Rayya has mastered and refashioned to uncon-
testable perfection."

There is not much a translator can add to that. Certainly, it is
a multidimensional novel, the characters are skillfully drawn, and
the small rural town is so well evoked that the sights, sounds, and
particularly the smells leap off the page to assault the senses. The

language of the novel is powerful, direct, tightly woven, and mixed: vivid colloquial Arabic is used for the dialog (except the 'translation' of conversations in sign language, which is given in standard Arabic), while colloquial usages—even ruralisms—also invade the standard Arabic of the narration. Of course, in an English translation, such stylistic variation can only occasionally be reflected.

I am grateful to the author, firstly for creating such a challenging and entertaining text to translate, and secondly for being there to answer my numerous questions, especially when it came to areas of life in which my experience was limited, such as butchery and hashish den culture.

My thanks also go to my friend Ahmed el-Barassi, who helped me on some linguistic issues in the early stages of the translation, and who then helped me maintain a distance by taking me away from my computer on long hikes in the deserts around the Fayoum.

My greatest debt of gratitude is to my inimitable friend Habiba Ahmed, who not only spent long evenings going over the text with me and untangling all the linguistic knots I was struggling with but constantly fed me into the bargain from her distinctive, eclectic, and delicious Egyptian, Moroccan, Hungarian, Indian, Fijian—and just plain Habiban—cuisine. Before and after dinner we pored, we discussed, and—as at all times, most importantly with Habiba—we laughed. This translation is dedicated with affection not only to Habiba but also to her husband Mohamed Noor and their daughter Nadia, who patiently put up with all this.

Although I finally read the whole text of the translation aloud as Habiba followed the Arabic to check for oversights or misunderstandings, any remaining errors are obviously my own.

Modern Arabic Literature
from the American University in Cairo Press

Ibrahim Abdel Meguid *Birds of Amber*
No One Sleeps in Alexandria • *The Other Place*
Yahya Taher Abdullah *The Mountain of Green Tea*
Leila Abouzeid *The Last Chapter*
Yusuf Abu Rayya *Wedding Night*
Ahmad Alaidy *Being Abbas el Abd*
Idris Ali *Dongola: A Novel of Nubia*
Ibrahim Aslan *The Heron* • *Nile Sparrows*
Alaa Al Aswany *The Yacoubian Building*
Hala El Badry *A Certain Woman* • *Muntaha*
Salwa Bakr *The Wiles of Men*
Hoda Barakat *Disciples of Passion* • *The Tiller of Waters*
Mourid Barghouti *I Saw Ramallah*
Mohamed El-Bisatie *Clamor of the Lake* • *Houses Behind the Trees*
A Last Glass of Tea • *Over the Bridge*
Fathy Ghanem *The Man Who Lost His Shadow*
Randa Ghazy *Dreaming of Palestine*
Gamal al-Ghitani *Zayni Barakat*
Tawfiq al-Hakim *The Prison of Life*
Yahya Hakki *The Lamp of Umm Hashim*
Bensalem Himmich *The Polymath* • *The Theocrat*
Taha Hussein *The Days* • *A Man of Letters* • *The Sufferers*
Sonallah Ibrahim *Cairo: From Edge to Edge* • *The Committee* • *Zaat*
Yusuf Idris *City of Love and Ashes*
Denys Johnson-Davies *The AUC Press Book of Modern Arabic Literature*
Under the Naked Sky: Short Stories from the Arab World
Said al-Kafrawi *The Hill of Gypsies*
Sahar Khalifeh *The Inheritance*
Edwar al-Kharrat *Rama and the Dragon* • *Stones of Bobello*
Betool Khedairi *Absent*
Ibrahim al-Koni *Anubis*
Naguib Mahfouz *Adrift on the Nile* • *Akhenaten, Dweller in Truth*
Arabian Nights and Days • *Autumn Quail* • *The Beggar*
The Beginning and the End • *The Cairo Trilogy: Palace Walk,*
Palace of Desire, Sugar Street • *Children of the Alley*
The Day the Leader Was Killed • *The Dreams* • *Echoes of an Autobiography*
The Harafish • *The Journey of Ibn Fattouma* • *Khufu's Wisdom*
Life's Wisdom • *Midaq Alley* • *Miramar* • *Naguib Mahfouz at Sidi Gaber*
Respected Sir • *Rhadopis of Nubia* • *The Search* • *The Seventh Heaven*
Thebes at War • *The Thief and the Dogs* • *The Time and the Place*
Wedding Song • *Voices from the Other World*